FIVE ROUNDABOUTS TO HEAVEN

John Bingham was born near York, the only son of the Sixth Baron Clanmorris, and educated at Cheltenham College and in France and Germany to learn the languages. After his return, he went to Yorkshire to join the *Hull Daily Mail* as a journalist and reported on everything from police courts, the tragedies of lost trawlers and murders to fires and flower shows. From there he was transferred to Fleet Street, where he worked on the old *Sunday Dispatch* as a reporter, picture editor and special writer.

Shortly before the outbreak of war he joined the Territorials in the Royal Engineers and was called up in 1939. After a brief spell in the Army, he moved to the Intelligence Service and worked in MI5 with Maxwell Knight, well known for his undercover work and for his studies as a naturalist.

After the war he spent two years in devastated Germany working in Hanover. A large part of this work involved distinguishing between genuine refugees from spies and infiltrators. He returned to England and was re-recruited by Maxwell Knight on a full-time basis.

His book *My Name is Michael Sibley* (also published by Penguin) was much acclaimed when it appeared in 1952. This was the first of a string of nearly twenty books all considered to be deeply understanding of murder in the context of human psychology. He has also written a factual book, *The Hunting Down of Peter Manuel* with the help of Detective Chief Superintendent William Muncie.

John Bingham is married to biographer and playwright Madeleine Bingham and is the father of writer Charlotte Bingham. Now retired, John Bingham lives in London and has a cottage in the Cotswolds.

John Bingham

FIVE ROUNDABOUTS
TO HEAVEN

PENGUIN BOOKS

Penguin Books Ltd, Harmondsworth, Middlesex, England
Viking Penguin Inc., 40 West 23rd Street, New York, New York 10010, U.S.A.
Penguin Books Australia Ltd, Ringwood, Victoria, Australia
Penguin Books Canada Limited, 2801 John Street, Markham, Ontario, Canada L3R 1B4
Penguin Books (N.Z.) Ltd, 182–190 Wairau Road, Auckland 10, New Zealand

First published by Victor Gollancz 1953
Published in Penguin Books 1959
Reissued 1986

Printed and bound in Great Britain by
Cox & Wyman Ltd, Reading
Typeset in Bembo

Chapter 1

I HAD been looking forward all day to the visit. Indeed, I had been looking forward to it ever since we had planned our trip to the south of France, and I had arranged the route so that we would pass through Orléans. It was a visit that I had wanted to make for a long time, a kind of pilgrimage to a shrine of happiness now suitably veiled in the rosy mists of youth.

Nineteen years is a long time. One cannot remember everything, and the tendency on occasions such as this is to remember only the happiness. The weather seems always to have been warm and sunny, the days filled with love and laughter, the nights throbbing with the notes of the nightingales in the woods, and, in my case, with the blithe croaking of the amorous frogs in the moat around the château.

If I concentrate hard enough, I can, of course, recall that there were minor irritations and frictions, but it is true to say that they never lasted long. We were all too young, too filled with the joy of living; and perhaps the mild and gentle air of the wooded Sologne country was itself an antidote to prolonged bitterness.

Even the pangs of youthful jealousy have a curious sweetness in retrospect, for with the near approach of middle age the emotions, in matters of the heart, tend to be flattened, and the ecstasies and agonies toned down.

One has seen it all before, perhaps many times: this, one says, is where I came in. And if one decides to see the show again, one knows how the reel will run, amiably anticipating the pleasant periods, suitably fortified against the pains and pangs. Such is the penalty and such is the protection which the years bring you.

What makes for happiness depends upon one's age. We,

who stayed at the château to learn French, were all young, of varied nationalities, and the road ahead seemed straight and sure, and to lead inevitably to a splendid fulfilment of such vague hopes for the future as we nurtured.

We had no doubts. We worked a little, we played tennis, gardened, and bathed in the lake in front of the château. In winter we went shooting. We fell in love, I need hardly add, some of us for the first time, and vowed undying faithfulness with all the confidence of extreme youth.

Our love was pure and idealistic, romantic and sweet. Looking back now, with a soul which is tarnished with dishonour and frayed round the edges, I am often amazed at this.

There was no hanky-panky at the château. And if I use a coarse music-hall expression in association with something which was fresh and beautiful, I ask you to be charitable, and to blame the span of the years and a half a working lifetime which has been spent in different parts of the world. One is inclined to become crude.

I have said that I am often amazed at the unsullied nature of our feelings, and that is strictly true: often, but not always. For now and again, like the memory of the scent of a rose-garden to some poor sufferer in a crowded town hospital, I catch a whiff of the fragrance of those earlier feelings, and I understand how we felt. A tune, such as 'My Blue Heaven', will naturally bring it back to me, or a particular type of perfume favoured by the young: but I may also catch it, suddenly and unexpectedly, walking along a street, or even in a crowded public-house. It had always been, hitherto, a thin wraith of the real thing, but I felt that if I went back to the château, saw it standing there, with its light-grey walls and blue shutters, at the end of the long drive of poplars, I would be able to recapture for a space not merely the full flavour of those past days, but also a glimpse of Philip Bartels as he then was.

I think I wanted to refresh my memory of the Bartels of those days almost as much as I wished to inflict upon myself the sweet pain of thinking of times now gone forever.

In spite of all that has happened, in spite of what Macdonald of Scotland Yard, and one or two others, have said, I still regard Bartels not only as my friend but as one of the most lovable characters I have ever known. Perhaps I, alone, understood what he felt.

*

All day, then, I had looked forward to this visit with a rising emotion, a physical disturbance of the stomach nerves, which amounted to veritable tension.

Two of the other three in our party knew nothing of the excitement within me; they thought of the excursion as only a casual visit to a familiar haunt. To them I must have seemed silent and broody that day. I was even asked, when I made a mere pretence of eating lunch, whether I felt quite fit.

Later that day I left them to stroll round Orléans, and took the car and drove through the little village of Verlin and out again to where the road was bordered by fields of corn, crisply brown and sprinkled with poppies and cornflowers.

The sun was at distant tree-top level when I pulled the car in to the side of the road, a few yards from the end of the poplar drive, and switched off the engine.

The evening was silent except for the creak of a cart on some distant farm and the far-away barking of a dog. The sky was cloudless. I climbed out of the car, and closed the door, and looked up and down the road. There was nobody in sight, and as I made my way towards the end of the avenue leading to the château the sound of my shoes upon the hard road seemed uncannily loud.

7

For a second I experienced one of those curious sensations in the course of which you wonder whether you are really alive, and then the feeling was past. I walked slowly, now that the fulfilment of my ambition was at hand, wishing to savour every minute, every second.

It was at first my plan to walk down the avenue, but at the last moment I decided against it. The family no longer lived there, and I had heard from one of the brothers that it was now the home of two families of American Air Force officers who were stationed in Orléans. They had set up a kind of communal cocktail bar in the entrance hall. If they were now sitting drinking on the terrace, they would be in a position to watch me walking down the long avenue and to speculate upon what I wanted.

I had no doubt that I would be hospitably received if I explained the nature of my visit, even though I was a stranger, but I did not wish to spend my precious time talking to other people, be they American, English, or French. My rendezvous was with the happy ghosts of the early 1930s, not with the worried flesh and blood of post-war years.

I turned aside, therefore, into the woods which pressed close upon the poplar-lined drive, following a path which I knew well from of old, which twisted and turned, but which eventually passed by the tennis-courts, and by the side of the house, and led to the rising ground on the other side of the château.

It was a path which Bartels and I had often taken to-gether, in the old days, when we wished to cross the Orléans-Blois highway to try for partridges on the land across the road. We preferred it to the avenue, for there was always the chance of a shot at a rabbit or a pigeon.

I trod it now, stepping as quietly as the leaves and twigs would permit, for the closer I came to the house the less I wished to be disturbed. Thus, stealthily, dreading equally

8

the querying word or friendly shout, I returned like a poacher to the scene of my happiness.

I passed the great rabbit-burrow, where we had once lost a ferret, and caught a glimpse, as I neared the house, of the cottage where grizzled old Georges Durois, the *garde de chasse*, used to live with his wife, Marie. Both are long since dead. (How he would grumble when I missed the rabbits which his ferret put out for my inexpert marksmanship!)

Then, close by the house, to the left of the path, I saw a weatherbeaten wooden hut and paused, for I did not recall it, though to judge by its appearance it had been there many years. It stood among some young trees, surrounded by brambles and other bushes, and appeared to serve no useful purpose.

I left the path to examine it more closely, but it was empty, rotting, a reminder of death and decomposition, and I turned away; but as I did so I caught a glimpse among the saplings of a sagging post with a metal handle, and looking more closely I saw near at hand some rusting wire-netting and another post, and knew that I looked upon all that remained of the tennis-courts.

Of all the laughter and youthful energy which this patch of ground had known, nothing now remained; it was just trees and brambles and a hut rotted by the weather.

The back of my throat ached, and I struck a match and lit my pipe. It was something to do, some physical action which might relieve the tension.

Behind me, in the wood, a pair of jays began to call harshly to each other; and above me, in a tall oak, I heard the vigorous rustling of a squirrel shaking the leaves. A descendant, I supposed of the squirrels I had known and sometimes shot, though always with reluctance, and only to please old Georges Durois; for of all the creatures which look ugly and pathetic dead, and pretty alive, squirrels head the list. I know they do harm, but the harm always seems to me negligible compared with the joy of seeing them about.

Then the jays ceased calling, and the squirrel moved to another tree, and except for the occasional whine of a mosquito the world was still.

I moved back to the path from the remains of the tennis-courts, and stood for a moment watching the bend in the path ahead. Surely Ingrid, my loved Ingrid, would come round the corner, in her pleated white tennis-skirt, radiating all the glory of her eighteen-years-old vitality; and behind her, plodding heavy-footed but purposeful, dear old slow-witted Danish Hans; and behind him, in a group, Mary, the vivacious little dark-eyed American girl; and Bob, the son of a Bradford wool merchant; and perhaps Freddie Harris, the ambitious cockney who worked in a bank and spent his annual holidays at the château to learn French and improve his prospects. And loping along to catch them up, always late, always gentle and good-tempered, would come any moment now old Rolf, the giant Norwegian with the build of an ancient Viking.

But not Philip Bartels. Not yet.

I didn't expect to see Bartels yet, for Bartels would be dressed in an old pair of flannel bags, and an open-necked shirt, sitting by the lake, trying for the fish he so rarely caught.

Then I realized that I was all wrong. It was now about seven o'clock. No wonder they didn't come. They would be changed for dinner, lounging on the terrace, in the soft evening sunshine, waiting for Madame to invite them into the dining-room. So I walked slowly on, more quietly than ever, and turned the bend and stood, partly concealed by a rhododendron bush, and gazed at the house.

It lay quite quiet and still, bathed in the waning sunlight, the walls glowing warmly, surrounded by the decorative moat. The little light wooden drawbridge, which one man could raise quite easily, was in position, connecting the terrace and the back of the château to the broad path which circled the reed-fringed lake and led to the drive between the poplars.

At the far side of the house I could see the hedge of the vegetable garden, where Madame had assigned a small plot of earth to those who wished for it; where I had grown the radishes. I was quite keen on keeping fit in those days, and used to get up at about 8.15 and put on a pair of shorts, and run a couple of times round the lake; and then go and pick some of my radishes.

I would wrap some of them in a handkerchief, and toss a pebble lightly against Ingrid's window, and when she put her head out, still tousled with sleep, I would throw them up to her. She used to like to eat them with her morning *petit déjeuner*. I looked at her window now, and then at the door below, leading to the terrace.

Apart from anything else, I knew from my correspondence with the family that Ingrid, whom I had lost, was married and living in Oslo; and loyal but slow-witted old Hans had found the Gestapo too much for him, and was dead. I did not know about Freddie, the bank clerk, but Bob had died at Alamein. And Mary, twice divorced, disillusioned, and hurt, was in Chicago.

But I peopled the terrace with my ghosts, just the same. I stood in the shadow of the rhododendron bush, and brought them all out, and made them stroll up and down and converse, and listened, from where I was, to the sound of their voices and to the occasional laughter.

Later, when I had had enough, I would allow them to drift into the house, and I would go to the most important rendezvous of all, to the place we called L'Étoile, because several paths converged there, so that it bore some resemblance to a star. There, Ingrid would come to meet me, as so often before, walking slowly through the woods with her hands clasped in front of her, arms at full length, a smile upon her face.

Looking back on that visit to the château now, seeing myself as I stood watching the empty house by the light of the dying sun, I agree that, at first, it was a pretty maudlin exhibition. I certainly piled it on a bit thick. I had come for sweet suffering, and I saw to it that I got it.

But then, though I fought against it, it all changed, and as the shadows lengthened the suffering was no longer sweet, but grim.

*

Some of the figures which I imagined once more upon the terrace were blurred, but Philip Bartels was clear enough.

We used to keep on the terrace one or more long, flexible rods, about six feet tall, which we cut from saplings. A length of thin string was tied to the top of each, and on the other end of the string was a little piece of red flannel. When we had five minutes to while away, we would lean over the side of the terrace and dangle the bit of flannel in front of the numerous frogs which lived in the moat. If a frog bit the flannel, mistaking it for a winged insect, we would whip it out of the water while its mouth was still entangled in the flannel, and then catch it in the grass by the side of the moat.

It didn't do the frogs any harm or us any good – only once did we decide to catch and kill enough to eat – and the skill lay in trying to deceive the frog by a life-like manipulation of the bait.

Bartels, the keen fisherman, was naturally the most enthusiastic. He would always stroll out in his dinner-jacket for a few minutes with the frogs before dinner. He was very good at frog-fishing. Sometimes Ingrid would lean over the terrace wall to watch him; and I would stroll out and join them both, because I was terribly jealous where Ingrid was concerned.

Bartels was my best friend. But Ingrid was my love. However, I realize now that I need not have worried. Knowing how I felt, Bartels was always scrupulously correct in his attitude to Ingrid.

All this I remembered, that wonderful summer night when I revisited the château: the château which was so quiet, and yet so alive to me who watched from the shadow of the rhododendron bush. I recalled, too, that the time came, many years later, when I myself was not so punctilious; when I acted craftily towards my best friend, with results which even to this day I find it difficult to assess.

I saw Bartels clearly that evening.

He stood out sharp-cut from the rest, leaning over the terrace wall. Once, he looked up and glanced for several long seconds towards where I stood, and so real did he seem that even now there are occasions when I wonder whether he was really summoned to the scene only by my imagination.

I saw him, a slenderly built figure of nineteen, with a lean face browned by the summer sun. He was not good-looking; indeed, in some ways there was something slightly comical about him. His features were reasonably regular, and the nose was straight and delicately chiselled; but he wore spectacles, of which the frames were of tortoiseshell and the side-pieces of gold; and although he kept his hair fairly well ordered, there were some hairs, on the crown of his head, which insisted upon sticking up. He had, too, a very wide mouth, of which the lips were rather thin and bloodless. So that sometimes, with his unruly hair and big mouth, he bore a faint resemblance to a cross between Donald Duck and one of the frogs he was so keen on catching.

I think his voice was his most attractive feature, that and his gentle, generous nature and ready sense of humour. His voice was deep and rich, and he always spoke very slowly and deliberately, and, when he looked towards me that evening, I seemed to hear him call to me, as he had often called before: 'Come and look here, Pete – there's a big one here going to bite!'

Yet although he was keen on gun and rod, I have seen him painstakingly rescue a drowning fly from a glass of wine, and place it on the window-ledge in the sun. On another occasion I saw him spend five minutes trying to manoeuvre a daddy-long-legs out of a window. And once, in the autumn, when a butterfly which had flown into the drawing-room fluttered into the fire, Bartels swung away from the grate with a gasp of horror, his hands over his face.

It was pain and suffering, for any living thing, which he abhorred, not death. He was unimpressed by death.

'What the hell difference do a few more days or years of life make in the limitless infinity of time?' he said once. 'Death is of no consequence. It only seems of consequence because people decline to recognize its inevitability. They fight against it, instead of accepting it for what it is, as normal an event as birth.'

I remember we were leaning over the terrace wall looking down at the frogs in the moat when he said it; one evening, it was, before dinner. He turned to go inside, but as he did so, he added:

'It's not dying that matters, it's how you die. It's the way in which you die.'

Hence the fly in the wine and the daddy-long-legs episodes; and his horror when the butterfly flew into the fire. Hence, too, the fact that he never took long, doubtful shots at wild game. He shot to kill.

He didn't mind killing. But it had to be in the right conditions. Pity and ruthlessness lay tranquilly together in his soul. A curious mixture, indeed.

That, then, was the Philip Bartels of those days.

I made my way round the house to the rising ground which faced that part of the drive which curved to the front door. I went to L'Étoile, and sat on a fallen tree-trunk, and waited as I had so often waited for Ingrid, in such a position that I could watch, between the trees, the front door through which she used to come to meet me.

But she didn't come.

She never came to me that evening. Instead, there was Bartels again, pushing the front door open, coming out and making his way towards me, his shotgun on his arm, a bag of cartridges over his shoulder.

I saw him pause and look back at the house; stand looking up at one of the windows, just as he paused and looked up at another window nearly twenty years later.

And I realized that the window he was looking at was the window of the room which Beatrice had occupied.

I remember very clearly the evening when Beatrice Wilson arrived. It was a July evening, and very hot, with that humid, sticky heat which is perhaps the sole disadvantage of the beautiful Sologne area. But now there were clouds gathering on the horizon, and every promise of the storm which would bring freshness and relief in its train.

Despite the heat, we had played tennis in the afternoon, had changed into evening dress and dined, and were sitting languidly on the terrace drinking coffee, when the family car which had fetched Beatrice from Orléans station swept round the drive to the front door. As always, we were filled with mild curiosity about the newcomer.

Those of us who were English had adopted other nationalities, in accordance with an innocent subterfuge dear to the heart of Madame. I was to pretend to be a Swede. This arrangement had two advantages: it removed from the newcomer the temptation to speak English, and it provoked a good deal of fun and many tricky situations, all of which encouraged French conversation.

I heard Madame greet Beatrice Wilson in the hall behind us, heard her go up to her room to wash. Then she came down and was introduced to us.

She was a lovely-looking girl of about eighteen. Slim, in those days, with red hair and the milk-and-roses complexion which goes with hair of that colour. Her features were regular and her eyes hazel. But I think that what impressed me most was her complete self-possession. She must have been aware that she was being summed up, by seven or eight young people, with all the critical and ruthless acumen of the young; yet so far from being disconcerted she appeared to be coolly indulging in some summing up herself. She gazed at each one of us in term, reflectively, as she was introduced, and when she spoke, she used her limited school French to the best advantage.

I formed the opinion that Beatrice Wilson was likely to be a pleasant acquisition to our company, and so it proved.

Two weeks after she arrived I had to leave, but Philip Bartels stayed on for another three months. By the time I left, I had mentally noted that now, instead of changing into old clothes and slouching off by himself to fish or shoot, Bartels had taken to changing into white flannels and was prone to join us on the tennis-courts in the afternoons. Moreover, it often chanced that he walked to and from the courts with Beatrice, and for tea and after-dinner coffee his chair was usually close to hers.

I was there to learn French because I was going into the hotel business; Bartels, because he was to join a well-known firm of wine importers; and Beatrice because her father, a solicitor in Worthing, thought that all his three children should be able to speak it.

I remember thinking, before I left, that Bartels might get

hurt, in the end, by the cool-headed Beatrice, because she did not seem to me to be the right type for him. I had no worse a premonition than that. But then I am not psychic. Not like Bartels' aunt Emily and aunt Rose, thank God.

I had come to the château that summer evening to dream only of the pleasant remote past, but instead, little by little, I found myself mentally drawing nearer and nearer to the events of a nearer date, of 26 February, that cold night of pain and anguish and fear. It was the last thing I wished; I was going on holiday to the south, partly, at least, to wipe out the memories of it all.

I suppose it happened because the events of February had occupied so much of my mind; so that even when I was not consciously thinking about the matter, it all lay there in my subconscious, ready to leap out and colour my thoughts, and even to some extent my actions.

For hours I would be free of the memories of that nightmare period, and then some little incident, some careless phrase from a stranger, perhaps, would bring me face to face with it; and off I would start, churning it all over and over again. Or perhaps the reason was that my own conscience was not clear in the matter.

Perhaps I had really come to the château, not so much from a nostalgic yearning for the scenes of youthful happiness, as I thought, nor even to meet again the image of my first love: else why did she not come when I sat on the log in the place called L'Étoile? Why was it Bartels whom my imagination summoned for me, if I did not feel the need for a final showdown with him?

But there I am wrong. The showdown was not to be with him. He always thought of me as his friend. The showdown was with myself.

*

I often wonder whether Bartels thought of me as he drove to London on the night of 26 February, with one eye on the dashboard clock and fear rising in his throat. I think he did.

If he didn't, he should have done, because I was responsible for his — what? I was about to write: because I was responsible for his downfall. But upon further reflection I think I could as well write that I was responsible for his salvation. It depends upon what you regard as salvation. I don't know for certain.

But I was certainly responsible for his fear. Terror, you could call it, just as you could consider his fear of enclosed spaces, of suffocation, to be terror.

I only saw two examples of it at the château. Once, during a visit to one or two of the more historic châteaux of the Loire, we stopped by the wayside for a picnic.

We spread some rugs in a field off the highway, and ate the food and drank the wine; and afterwards lay about for a while, smoking and talking and joking. In due course, one or two of the more active spirits began to lark about.

I think it was Danish Hans who crept up behind Bartels and flung a rug over his head and held him tight within its folds. I shall never forget the wild struggle which ensued, the sight of Bartels' thrashing arms and legs, the upsetting of the wine-bottle and picnic utensils, and, when he finally released himself, Bartels' eyes, at first wild with terror and then hot and angry.

'Don't ever do that again,' he said, and got up and walked some distance away and sat down by himself. We looked at each other silently, as people often will who find themselves in the presence of something they don't understand. Nobody said anything. And in due course, though still somewhat subdued, we went upon our way.

The other occasion was when we were playing some hide-and-seek kind of game one evening. Somebody, I forget whom, knowing that Mary and Bartels were hiding together in a bedroom, locked the door on them, proposing to make a joke of it later, and to tell Bartels that he would have to marry the girl now.

But it didn't work out that way.

We had to unlock the door almost at once in answer to the terrible, incessant banging upon it, and the unnaturally high-pitched shouts of Philip Bartels from within.

Later, I asked Mary what had happened, but she wouldn't discuss it. She just said; 'I don't think he likes being locked in. Some people have that fear. Claustrophobia, or something.'

She quickly changed the subject. I formed the impression that what she had seen had been so upsetting that she did not wish to talk about it.

Chapter 2

I AM, I believe, the only person who is in a position to record the full facts about Philip Bartels. One other person thinks he knows them, but he doesn't. For one thing, he doesn't know that I am, I suppose, a murderer, and one who carried out his crime under the nose of a police officer who, to this day, is quite unaware of the fact.

I know the facts because I was so intimately acquainted with all the people in the affair. I still am, for that matter, but for obvious reasons I have used fictitious names for everybody, including myself. Indeed, especially for myself, for I am nothing if not prudent.

The reconstruction of the story, then, is simple enough, but I may, I suppose, be attacked for daring to portray the thoughts which went on in the mind of Philip Bartels. How, I may be asked, do I know what went on in his mind?

I might defend myself by saying that I knew Bartels better than anybody else ever knew him; that I knew his mind better than I knew the mind of any of my other friends; that twenty-eight years is a long time to know anybody.

But I must record, with respect, and without in any way wishing to appear rude, that I am largely indifferent as to whether I am attacked or not.

That is because – and here again I state the fact with the utmost diffidence – I am recording this business mostly for my own benefit; for my own peace of mind, perhaps. I myself did not play a noble role, and I want to get it all down on paper.

I, Peter Harding, am a proprietor of hotels, comparatively young, but comparatively successful, and I am used to having things down on paper. I like it that way. I don't like carrying things in my head.

One other thing I know, now that the visit to the château is past: although I went there at first from nostalgic and other reasons, I hadn't been there long before I realized that I was edging closer and closer to a solution to the one problem which had always baffled me: why a man of Bartels' nature acted as he did.

I shall never forget my feeling of rising excitement as, little by little, I drew nearer to the answer to the last riddle surrounding the strange personality of Philip Bartels.

Chapter 3

ALL living things need love. Even plants reach up for the caresses of the sun's rays. Children and young people need it more than others, so that affection and a sense of security, though important, are no substitute for the real thing. I think that Bartels craved love in later days because, unlike myself, he was starved of it an an early age.

I first met him when we were ten years old and day-boys at a little school in York. Then, as later, he was no beauty. He was a little frog-faced chap, with gold-rimmed spectacles: and then, as later, he was of only medium height, and weedily built. During his first two terms he was badly bullied, and I took part in the bullying, and thought it rather fun.

We used to roll him up in the matting in the gymnasium and bounce on him. There was a piano in the gymnasium, too, and singing lessons took place there, and sometimes, for a change, we would poke him under the vaulting-horse and keep him there the entire lesson.

Some psychologists say that if you know the cause of irrational fears you are as good as cured. Bartels suffered in after life from claustrophobia, which he ascribed to the vaulting-horse incidents: but the knowledge didn't cure him.

When school was over, we would lie in wait for him outside the premises, but after a while he grew to expect this, and would lurk about in the comparative safety of a classroom until time compelled us to go home. I remember to this day the sight of his pale little face pressed against the classroom window as he waited hopefully for us to leave. Poor little Bartels!

After a couple of terms we gave up bullying him, principally because he was a good-humoured fellow, and he and I became firm friends.

At that time my parents had rented a house at Dringhouses, on the outskirts of York. There was a field next door in which black pigs were kept and a stagnant pond. After I had stopped bullying Bartels, we united to bully the pigs by throwing mud balls at them: and occasionally, since this was soon after the First World War, we would play at naval battles with bits of wood on the pond.

During our last term at the school a play was produced in which I had the role of Julius Caesar and Bartels played Cassius. It used to amuse us greatly when I had to speak the famous words:

> Let me have men about me that are fat;
> Sleek-headed men and such as sleep o' nights.
> Yond Cassius has a lean and hungry look;
> He thinks too much: such men are dangerous.

It never occurred to me then that Bartels could ever be a dangerous man. Even in those days he was such a kind-hearted and gentle chap.

For instance, we used to play a ludicrous card game called 'Lams and Biffs', in which we gambled, not for money but for our personal comfort or discomfort. At the end of the game, various winners inflicted upon various losers a number of whacks with a ruler to equal the points they had gained. Nobody much minded losing to Bartels, because you always got off with a few soft, perfunctory pats.

When we left the little school in York, we went to different preparatory schools, and later, to different public schools, but I still saw a tremendous lot of him in London, during the school holidays.

My parents had a modernized flat in Kensington, and because they were gay and interested in everybody, and content with their lot, there was always a joke or two in the evenings, and a friend popping in for a talk and a cup of coffee.

But for Bartels it was different.

He was just thirteen when both his parents were killed in a train crash in France, and he was compelled to go and live with his aunt Emily, her sister, aunt Rose, and his uncle James, a retired colonel of the Somerset regiment, who, in addition to other acts of bravery, had married Bartels' aunt Rose.

I have come across some quaint households in my time, but nothing that could beat the extraordinary set-up into which Philip Bartels, a lonely and sensitive child, was pitchforked at the impressionable age of thirteen.

There was laughter enough in my home, but the only jokes which amused me when I visited Bartels were quite unintentional and entirely due to the farcical goings-on in that incredible place.

As for friends popping in for a chat, any acquaintances who called, for one reason or another, took their departure as soon as decency permitted, and I don't blame them.

Yet they were not wicked people. All the people in this record were fundamentally good people, apart from myself, perhaps; which possibly makes the tale of some slight interest, for crime involving wicked people is common enough.

Bartels' relations were kind and generous. They were very fond of each other, too, and would have given their last stick of furniture to help each other in case of dire emergency. But they were so occupied with the affairs of this world – and indeed of the next world, too – that they had little time to lavish upon Bartels the love which a child needs.

I got to know them well over the years, for I was an only child and glad enough to go round there two or three times a week in the holidays. In the end, I even called them aunt

Rose, and uncle James, and aunt Emily, as though they were my own relations.

The house in which Bartels lived was situated off Bayswater Road, its exact address being No 257 Melville Avenue.

The word conjures up a double row of trees, but if there had ever been any trees in Melville Avenue they must have been long since chopped down, or, more likely, have died of blight. In either case it must have been a merciful release for them.

There was no real colour in Melville Avenue. The houses, each hugging its neighbour, each with its two stucco pillars on either side of a flight of steps, were painted in tones which appeared to have been primarily chosen for their drabness. Some were fawn, some grey, and some had their pillars painted a curiously depressing shade of chocolate brown, or even black. The house owned by aunt Emily had once been painted the shade of weak mustard.

Behind each house was a small garden, bordered by a grimy brick wall, and here lurked various dark-leaved shrubs and trees. Some house-owners tried to grow a patch of lawn – Bartels' uncle had tried to do so – but the earth was black and sour and full of broken bricks and stones, and the grass grew only thinly and coarsely.

At No 257 the square of rank grass, with its bald patches and ragged edges, had been surrounded by Bartels' aunt Rose with a border of large sea-shells, which made it particularly repulsive. Along the wall at the end of the garden an endless procession of cats passed by day and by night. Some were tabby, some black, some tortoiseshell or white, and a few displayed such a variety of colour and design as to make the imagination boggle at the broadmindedness of their ancestors.

No 257 Melville Avenue, like all the neighbouring houses, had a ground floor and basement, and two other stories. Bartels' aunt Rose, and her husband James, aunt Emily, Cook, and Bartels himself occupied the ground floor and basement.

The first floor was let to a retired District Commissioner from East Africa, whose name I have forgotten. I would sometimes see him and his wife passing down the stairs, a spare, yellow-faced, unhappy-looking couple. He had obtained a job as secretary in some minor West End club, and rarely returned until late at night.

Now and again, when my parents went away, I would spend a night at Bartels' house; and I would hear the wife's footsteps, as I lay in bed, pacing backwards and forwards, backwards and forwards, above my head. Once I heard sobbing. I think she was being driven mad by loneliness.

The top floor was let to an artist in his early thirties, and the woman whom he called his wife, though sometimes, carelessly readdressed letters led aunt Rose to remark good-humouredly that if Mrs Martin were asked to produce her marriage lines she might be hard put to it to find them. The Martins were a gay and happy couple, who kept much to themselves.

Sometimes they gave noisy parties which went on late into the night, and afterwards the guests would make their way on tip-toe, giggling and whispering, down the lino-leum-covered stairs. I have sometimes wondered how the District Commissioner's wife felt, as she listened to the sounds of gaiety, so near and yet so far removed from her.

*

Aunt Rose and uncle James, as from force of habit I still think of them, lived on the ground floor with Bartels; aunt Emily and Cook lived in the basement. It is typical of the remarkable salesmanship of aunt Rose that although aunt Emily owned the house, aunt Rose and her husband occupied the best rooms, though they paid no rent, while aunt Emily lived in the basement.

The reason was clear enough, at least to aunt Rose, and lay in the fact that one day aunt Rose was going to be a millionairess, and was going to keep all the rest of the family in luxury for the remainder of their lives.

All that stood between her and untold riches – computed at compound interest, the figure ran into hundreds of millions – was the little matter of winning a law-suit against her husband's cousin. It was known as Aunt Rose's Case, and was a subject of incessant discussion.

It was a case with such tortuous ramifications that though I heard it explained a dozen times, though talk of it interrupted on countless occasions my evening games with Bartels, I never really got the hang of it.

I only know it was full of legitimate and illegitimate births, of stolen birth certificates, pages torn out of church registers, wicked sisters, old family nurses who remembered this, and old chief clerks who remembered that; all of whom were prepared to go into the witness-box and swear that this or that did or did not happen.

True, one lawyer after another had turned the case down, or quarrelled with aunt Rose. This one had apparently been too weak; that one bribed by the opposition; a third intimidated; a fourth had had the audacity to demand some interim payment.

Invariably, when I returned for the holidays, she had at last found the right man, a real fighter, honest and unafraid of anybody. By Jove, he was going to make them sit up! The writs were going out next week, if Counsel's opinion were favourable! But it never was.

Bartels' aunt Rose was a short woman with fair hair, grey eyes, and a belligerent disposition, and prone to emphasize her words by pounding the table with her fist; in contrast, aunt Emily was tall, with a pale oval face, wide, dark, credulous eyes, and an earnest, anxious expression; she wore old-fashioned inexpensive jewellery, odd bits of lace and fur, and in her ears a pair of long black ear-rings.

There was one snag about aunt Rose's law-suit: there was always a bit of money which had to be paid out for something or other.

Uncle James had long since commuted his Army pension and had only a small family allowance left. So aunt Rose used to fall back upon aunt Emily for financial assistance.

I have often wondered whether aunt Rose was a rogue or a misguided woman, and have come to the conclusion that if she twisted aunt Emily out of every penny she could get out of her, which she did, she probably thought that she was really acting in the true interests of everybody. (Even I myself, though no blood relation, was going to benefit financially in some obscure way no longer clear to me, once the great case was won.)

Had she not a case which was just on the point of coming to Court, which when won – and who could doubt it would be won! – would enable her to repay aunt Emily every penny she had had from her, including the years of unpaid rent, and enable everybody to buy rich estates in the country and live happily ever after?

The links in the chain were complete, except for one or two paltry bits of evidence which would come to hand at any moment. Who, then, should more properly finance her for a further few months than aunt Emily, who stood to gain so much?

Sometimes aunt Emily was a bit sticky about paying up. You could scarcely blame her. On such occasions the glass and the letters of the alphabet would come out at aunt Rose's suggestion.

Everybody knew Bartels' aunt Rose was psychic, because she said so herself, over and over again. Aunt Emily thought that she, too, was psychic, but she would admit in an awed tone that she was not nearly as psychic as aunt Rose.

So in due course, if her sister was being difficult about money, aunt Rose would arrange the letters in a circle around the little, highly polished mahogany table, and place the glass in the middle, and they would both place the tips of their fingers lightly on the upturned glass.

Thus they would sit in silence for a few moments; aunt Rose, untidily dressed, but intense and forceful; and aunt Emily dressed in her eternal bits and pieces, and black ear-rings, her cow-like eyes, utterly credulous, fixed watchfully on the glass.

Fortunately the spirits never kept them waiting long, largely because they knew, no doubt, that aunt Rose had so much work to do on her case.

I remember the last time I ever saw aunt Rose at work. It was a remarkably fine exhibition.

Aunt Emily had said she had not a penny more to spare for the moment. Not a penny. So after a tactful interval aunt Rose suggested having a turn with the glass. Aunt Emily could never resist it, though she ought to have known by bitter experience exactly what was going to be the end of it.

After the usual short wait, aunt Emily said, in her nervous way:

'Is anybody there? Who is there?'

For a second or two the glass remained immobile while aunt Emily stared raptly into space, her face twisted into the sort of welcoming smile which she imagined a spirit on a short visit to Bayswater might find reassuring. Then the tumbler began to move hesitatingly from letter to letter and spelt out: F-A-T-H-E-R.

'It's Father!' cried aunt Rose triumphantly. He was I may add, a frequent astral caller at the Bayswater house.

'Well, well,' said aunt Emily, trying to keep her voice

normal, 'what do you want, Father? Are you and Mother happy?'

The glass, gaining confidence, moved quickly.

'Y-U-S,' spelt out aunt Emily in a puzzled tone.

'He means "Yes",' whispered aunt Rose, quickly separating the U and the E a little more, and replacing her fingers on the glass.

'B-U-T,' said Father, 'I A-M,' and paused to think.

'What are you, Father?' asked aunt Emily.

'W-A-R-R-I-E-D.'

'Warried?' Aunt Emily looked at aunt Rose.

'Worried,' said aunt Rose. 'Father's worried. Why are you worried, Father?'

At this stage, aunt Emily should have been the one to be worried, but she never was. She just rushed blindly on to her fate. The answer was always the same:

'R-O-S-E'S C-A-S-E.'

'Rose's Case,' said aunt Rose, and gave her sister a significant look. It was too late for aunt Emily to back out now without gross disrespect to the dead.

'H-E-L-P,' said Father succinctly, and added: 'C-A-S-E W-I-L-L B-E W-O-N S-O-O-N.'

'Isn't that wonderful!' whispered aunt Rose. But that was not the end; the sting was in the tail, and the glass now moved quickly and surely.

'M-O-N-E-Y N-E-E-D-E-D F-A-M-I-L-Y M-U-S-T S-T-A-N-D F-O-U-R S-Q-U-A-R-E T-O-G-E-T-H-E-R.'

'How shall we get the money, Father?' asked aunt Emily though she ought to have known. Father seemed to try tactfully to side-step this for a moment, as though to break it gently. He just said: 'F-I-G-H-T S-H-O-U-L-D-E-R T-O S-H-O-U-L-D-E-R,' and was silent. It was as though he were brooding deeply over the whole problem.

Then, apparently having made up his mind, he added starkly: 'E-M-I-L-Y M-U-S-T S-E-L-L S-O-M-E S-H-A-R-E-S.'

Perhaps because he saw the blank look on aunt Emily's face he added: 'I-F N-E-C-E-S-S-A-R-Y.'

Just occasionally, my parents visited the house, and, once, a rather half-hearted attempt was even made to bounce some money out of my father, but being cynical he remained deaf to astral instructions and no further efforts were made.

Although I never felt sorry for Bartels' aunt Rose, with her buoyant optimism and continual preoccupation with her great case, I did feel a certain pity for uncle James, her husband, the man around whom the whole case revolved.

He never struck me as having the air of a man who seriously considered himself to have been gravely wronged; indeed, he seemed to regard both the case and the astral messages with a certain good-humoured tolerance. But he was always very cagey when questioned as to his views on both subjects, probably because he held aunt Rose in some awe.

He was a short, well-proportioned man dressed invariably in the style of a country gentleman who had come up to spend an hour or two at Tattersall's.

He wore loud check suits, usually grey, made of heavy cloth of such superb quality that though they had been made in the late Edwardian period they still looked new; and on him, somehow, the style still looked smart. He always wore white socks, and, outside the house, grey spats, a brown bowler hat, and carried yellow gloves; his shoes shone like a well-polished Sheraton table. He had fair, thinning hair, a square jaw and straight nose, and keen, merry blue eyes.

One evening I saw uncle James's car in front of the house; he was polishing the coachwork, whistling and hissing through his teeth like an ostler does when rubbing a horse down after a gallop. It was a very old car, but Bartels' uncle kept it shining like a new pin.

'Hello, uncle James,' I said. He looked up.

'Hello, Peter!' He roared with laughter. He had the social habit common to his generation of going off into peals of loud laughter if he met somebody unexpectedly.

'How are you?' he said in his loud, cheerful voice. 'Phil's out at the moment, but he'll be back soon.'

We chatted for a while and then made our way to the dreary expanse of coarse grass and dark green foliage behind the house, and walked up and down, discussing the sort of garden he would like to have, the vagaries of his car, and the scarcity of .money, while a grimy-looking tabby cat sat on the wall dreaming of the infinite.

'How's the case?' I asked at length.

'I believe Rose is up to some new dodge or other. This new lawyer fella was no good after all. Ah, well, it's a poor heart that never rejoices,' he added.

'It certainly is.'

'I'd like to have a day out hunting before I die, I must say. I get tired of being the poor relation, Pete.'

He paused to light his pipe, sucking in the smoke with short, vigorous puffs, so that in a few seconds there was a thick cloud of acrid blue smoke around him.

It seemed odd that a man who had had charge of the destinies of a great regiment, who had been a local god to a thousand men, should be pacing up and down a seedy garden in Bayswater, dreaming of one last day out with the hounds before he died. He longed for a job, and it seemed to him bewildering that though he was over sixty, and untrained in anything except war, nobody would offer him one.

To the end of his days he never gave up hope, either of a job or of a last day's hunting. He got neither, of course.

Uncle James helped daily with the housework, tended the garden, carried the coals, chopped wood, cleaned the shoes, and pressed his own clothes; he was always as immaculately clean as in the days when a batman had looked after him.

When she occasionally grew fretful about handing out money in accordance with Father's wishes from Beyond, aunt Emily would sometimes suggest that her sister's one spare room could be used to house a rich lodger. Doubtless she envisaged some old recluse, full of years and money, who would eventually die and leave them his fortune. But aunt Rose said it would be 'bad for James's nerves', not that he was ever known to suffer from any.

Looking back now over the years, I see they were a cheerful, feckless couple who wasted their substance chasing a mirage; who fed well, and were never without a bottle of whisky in the house; who ran up bills which they could not pay, and believed that the world owed them a living.

But they were sweethearts from the day they met until the day when death came to aunt Rose, and the dustman eventually carted away the vast accumulation of papers in the case that aunt Rose never won, and never could have won, had she lived to be a hundred.

*

I smile when I think of them, Bartels' aunt Rose, aunt Emily, and uncle James; time has erased from the memory such blemishes of character as they may have had, and wiped out the recollections of the inevitable little acrimonious squabbles which arose between them.

They were kind to Philip Bartels, they were genuinely fond of him, but that is as far as it went. Aunt Emily was too occupied with her stocks and shares and her tenants, and aunt Rose was too occupied fighting the legal scoundrel, and rogues who declined to work for her without payments to develop any real love of him.

Even uncle James never really took to him, for Bartels had never hunted, never showed much interest in the Army

33

as a career, and at that time did not know one end of a shot-gun from another.

That, then, was the boyhood background of the man the cool-brained Beatrice married, the girl whose arrival at the château was followed, appropriately, as it now seems, by one of the most violent thunderstorms in the history of the Sologne area.

Few lives are completely tragic or even sombre. Bartels' boyhood had its amusing side, even its ludicrous moments, but he was too young fully to appreciate them.

In retrospect his youth seems, on the whole, not un-pleasant. There have been many worse. But it did him no good, no good at all. Bartels needed more emotional warmth than he could ever find at 257 Melville Avenue; more, too, than Beatrice Wilson could ever give him, either before or after they were married.

Chapter 4

BROODING *in the woods above the château where Bartels and I had been so happy, I was compelled to admit to myself that I had played my cards cleverly in the events which occurred all those years later.*

I concealed my part in the Bartels' affair so well that I know for certain that on the February night when, for him, the world burst into flames and fell in ruins, the thoughts which he entertained for me were still those of a friend.

His actions proved it.

So much the better. I am glad to think that to the burden of his fear there was not added the bitterness of one who thinks he has been betrayed.

I don't say that the role I played was a noble one. It was not. Where things of the heart are concerned men mostly become selfish. But although my actions had been dictated by my own interests, I had for long been in doubt as to whether I need entirely reproach myself for the course which I took.

I had argued that I had acted, at first, perfectly legitimately, and that by the time the moment for sacrifice had arrived, only a saint could have found the strength to make it.

If you lead a normal life in a town such as London, if you can call town life normal, which I doubt, you can get away from your conscience to some extent. I could, anyway. There are plenty of distractions.

But it was different when I was back there that evening.

When you go back, as I did, and see the ghosts, and one ghost in particular, and see him as he was, and remember all that happened in later years, you come face to face with yourself.

Arguments which had formerly held good begin to fall away. Doubts creep in, slimily, from behind, and you've got to round on them and grab them by the throat and throttle them, if you can, or they trample you down.

So the truth begins to emerge.

Chapter 5

AFTER I had left the château I went to Germany and Italy, to learn the languages of those countries. I worked in hotels at home and abroad, on the Continent and in America, for although my father had a comfortable position in mind for me when I knew the hotel business, he was determined that I should go through the mill first.

I worked in every department which you can find in a big hotel, doing both manual work and office work, for my father, who had built his business the hard way, had no mind to have it wrecked some day by a dilettante.

It was hard, but I enjoyed it, meeting many types of men, and almost as many different types of women. But I rarely stayed more than a few months in each place, and, since there is safety in numbers, the attractions of one girl had hardly begun to impress me before I left; and the charms of her successor, I must own, proved scarcely less acceptable.

I had lost Ingrid, for reasons which it is unnecessary to outline, and thereafter I remained comparatively free.

It was not so with Bartels.

We wrote to each other fairly often, and in due course I learnt that he had gone into the wine trade, as envisaged, that after a period in a London office he had toured the well-known vineyards, and finally he had gone out on the road to sell his wares.

It is not fair to mention here the name of the firm for which he worked, but it had a reasonable reputation, and with the small income he inherited from his parents, and what he made by way of commission, he had an adequate income, at the age of twenty-six, upon which to marry.

So he married. He married Beatrice Wilson, and invited me formally to the wedding, though I was at that time in

America. And when I heard the news I wondered why Beatrice Wilson, that attractive, witty, and intelligent girl, should have married little frog-faced Bartels; even though he did have a certain charm, and a slow and melodious voice.

I spent most of the war in a Japanese prisoner-of-war camp, but I was lucky, and returned to London in comparatively good health, in 1946. As my parents were at that time living in Buckinghamshire, I sought and was fortunate enough to find a small modern furnished flat in Kensington High Street, and soon after my return, I telephoned Bartels at his office, not knowing whether he was dead or alive.

There was no mistaking the slow, deep voice, which answered the phone, and which contrasted so curiously with his slender frame. He sounded genuinely delighted to hear from me. I agreed to go to dinner with him and Beatrice the following night, and when we learnt that we were living within a few minutes' walk of each other we were as pleased as Punch.

It seemed that our old boyhood friendship would be renewed, and indeed for three years and more this proved to be the case. It was a happy time for me. I had work, friends, my darkroom in my flat, where I carried out photographic experiments.

I was delighted to see that, despite certain misgivings I had had, to all outward appearances the marriage was a success.

Beatrice was a splendid housewife. She was still extremely good-looking and seemed contented and happy. Her parents had bought for her a small cottage near Balcombe, in Sussex, and in the summer months they would go down there for long week-ends. I often went with them.

They had a pleasant circle of friends, both in London and

in Sussex, and if I sometimes thought that Bartels was quieter than he used to be, I formed the opinion that this was because he had not been very well treated by his firm.

It was, of course, the old story of the man who goes to the war – in his case, the African campaign, Italy, and Germany – and who returns to find that others have been promoted in his absence. They gave him his job back – on the road – but they pointed out, with a regret which might have been genuine, that in the present state of the wine trade they could do no more.

Bartels was not as young as he had been, and I think he felt it deeply. Moreover, good wine was not, at first, easily obtainable; and at first, being expensive, was difficult to sell.

But Beatrice had a small allowance for her clothes, and Bartels had his modest private income, so that despite everything they managed to live reasonably. Bartels, who was of Dutch origin as his name suggests, stuck tenaciously to his selling, even though it involved an absence from home of two or three nights a week.

I spent very many happy evenings with the Bartels and with their friends. There was Fred Manders, who was an architect, and his wife, Joyce; James Murray, an insurance chap; Bill and Margaret Barnet – he was something in a textile firm; and in the country there were the Derbyshires, who had a small-holding which they farmed in a desultory kind of way; Major and Mrs Godfrey, who did nothing in particular; John O'Brien, an Irish solicitor, who lived near by in a cottage by himself and travelled up and down to town each day, and one or two others. Of them all, I liked John O'Brien best. He was a heavily built, jovial man in his middle thirties, with dark hair and blue eyes and a pugnacious jaw.

When I first met him he was already contemplating taking silk, and I formed the impression, and later events confirmed it, that with his good looks and Irish charm and wit he would go far at the Bar.

He lived in the country, primarily because he was passionately devoted to St Bernard dogs, of which he had three. I frequently gave him a lift to town in my car, and on Sundays, when the Bartels were down there, he generally came in for a meal or a few drinks.

We all liked John O'Brien. I still do.

I had an open invitation to go down to Balcombe any week-end I liked, with or without warning. All that I needed to do, they said, was to drive up to the door. I often did. My room was always ready. Such was the closeness of the bonds between myself and Philip and Beatrice Bartels.

So things remained for a period, which in retrospect seems like that sunny windless day when Beatrice arrived at the château and entered the life of Philip Bartels; the day which ended, so suddenly, in the gathering of the storm-clouds and the rending of the sky by thunder and lightning and rain.

Even when the first crack appeared, I was, at first, merely surprised and saddened. It began on 12 February, when he telephoned me at my office, and invited me to lunch at the Café Royal, saying that he had something he wished to tell me.

I was rather busy that morning, and tried to stall him off.

'It all depends upon what you want to tell me,' I remember I answered cautiously.

He hesitated. 'It is something you ought to know,' he replied at last.

'Can't you make it tomorrow? I've got a hell of a lot of work to cope with.'

'It's no good tomorrow. I really do want to see you to-day, alone.' Although he spoke in that slow, strong voice which contrasted so much with his appearance, I detected a note of genuine urgency in his tones.

'All right,' I said. 'I'll come.'

'See you in the cocktail lounge at one o'clock – upstairs. No, make it twelve-thirty.'

'Don't be silly. I told you I've got a lot of work.'

'It'll be pointless if you don't come at twelve-thirty.'

I hesitated again. 'What the hell is it about?'

'I can't tell you on the phone.'

I thought: Oh well, I suppose I can make up the time this evening.

'All right, then. Twelve-thirty. I hope it's worth it, that's all.'

'It'll be worth it. I'm glad you can make it. It's very important to me, Peter. I want your opinion.'

I took a taxi, and arrived very punctually, but he was already seated on one of the settees, and had ordered my usual gin and tonic.

Looking at him, as I walked towards him, I thought he had not changed much over the years. He was still meagrely built, whereas I had put on too much weight. There was the same wide, gentle smile. But recently he had seemed more withdrawn, at any rate when in the company of people other than myself; ironically, he trusted me, implicitly.

When with other people there was a faintly enigmatic air about him. In addition to his slow, deliberate, almost tired way of speaking, he had acquired an equally deliberate way of thinking for some seconds before answering a question; and while he was thinking, he would sometimes look at you with a sardonic smile, not on his lips or even in his eyes – it was not as noticeable as that – but rather behind his eyes. It was as if he were amused, not at you, but at certain remote implications behind your question.

I put it down to the experiences, the rebuffs, which he had had 'on the road'. He was not a very successful traveller for his wine firm. Had he not had a private income, he would have been hard put to it to live as he did.

The impression you had, in those days, was of one who had schooled himself to accept the disappointments of life with a kind of amused contemplation. It was as though he were patiently awaiting the end of some phase or other, before proceeding on to some unspecified destiny.

It was a queer sort of attitude, and I should say that it was hardly conducive to persuading hard-bitten wine merchants to part with their money.

He joined me in a vague toast to our mutual good health, and said nothing for some moments, but sat picking at a cigarette end in the ash-tray with a used match. I asked him how business was, and he said it might be worse.

I looked around the room, knowing it was useless to hurry him.

The place was filling up rapidly. Across the room three bald men were drinking cocktails. They were obese, and sat huddled forward, round a little table, their knees apart to ease the weight of their stomachs. They were animated and joking, and at the all-jolly-good-fellows stage. Later, the masks would drop, and they would get down to business.

Suddenly Bartels asked me about his wife. It was the last sort of question I anticipated.

He said: 'Do you like Beatrice? I mean are you fond of her?'

'Of course I like her,' I said. 'Of course I'm fond of her. She's a dam' good scout. Why?'

He nodded, as though he expected the answer, as well he might have done; you are hardly likely, whatever you think, to tell your best friend that you dislike his wife.

'What are you getting at?' I asked.

'I'm fond of her, too. That's the devil of it.'

'A lot of men are quite fond of their wives. I'm told it's a mild kind of complaint, like chickenpox. You'll probably get over it. But it may take time.'

He didn't smile. He looked across the room and said: 'Well, I'm going to leave Beatrice, Peter. I thought I had better tell you. I thought you ought to know.'

I have always prided myself on not showing dismay. I admire the Roman Catholic priest who said in the Confessional: 'You have committed murder, my son? Well, how many times?' So I took a pull at my gin and tonic, and replaced the glass on the table, and said as casually as I could:

'Oh? Why? Why are you going to leave Beatrice?'

'Because I want to be happy.'

'That's reasonable.'

He gulped down his drink, and signalled to the waiter. But I said: 'This one is on me,' and gave the order, though my own glass was still half full. When the waiter had taken the order I asked the obvious question:

'Well, what's her name?'

'What's whose name?'

I knew he was fencing, and he knew that I knew it. I suppose it was a kind of conventional approach.

'The name of the woman you've fallen for,' I said. 'I know you and Beatrice well enough to know that your marriage is not an unhappy one. As a matter of fact, as marriages go, I always thought it was rather satisfactory. Who is she? And do I know her?'

'Lorna is her name,' said Bartels, still fiddling with the matchstick. 'Lorna Dickson. You haven't met her.'

I said nothing. When I said that I was fond of Beatrice, I was speaking the strict truth; and when Bartels said that he was still very fond of her, I knew that he was speaking the truth, too. Beatrice had turned into a fine character. She

43

was intelligent and witty; loyal to her own people; conscientious and hard-working; she obviously had a passionate disposition; and with it all, she was, as I've said, still remarkably good-looking in a red-haired, fair-skinned sort of way. She was also a really first-class cook.

So that all in all, I couldn't see that Bartels had much to grumble about.

It seemed to me perfectly clear that this Dickson woman was a floosy who had caught Bartels on the hop, at that period of a marriage when one or other of the partners is often ripe for a change. I had seen more intelligent, more sober-minded men than Bartels go down before that sort of thing; and live to regret it, too. But I knew it would be bad tactics to show opposition.

'Is she very good-looking?' I asked.

'To me, she is. To me she is beautiful. Other people might not think so.'

Still continuing on my tack of showing no fundamental opposition I said: 'Well, if you feel deeply enough, you'll have to do as you plan. Beatrice will take it hardly.'

'You don't need to tell me that.'

'No doubt she'll get over it,' I said.

'No doubt.'

A silence fell between us.

The waiter brought the second round of drinks. When he had given me my change and gone, I said:

'How long have you known Laura?'

'Lorna's her name.'

'Well, Lorna, then.'

'About four months.'

'Sometimes these things pass, you know.'

Bartels turned and looked at me, and said: 'This won't. This is the real thing.'

Having kicked around the world a bit, I suppose I have rather a mixed conception of morality. I am quite prepared, on occasions, to argue that the end justifies the means, and I was fond of Beatrice. I thought she was in for a pretty raw deal.

So I said: 'Why not hang on a little longer? Why not have Lorna, if you wish, as – well, as your girl friend? Just to make sure.'

'You mean as my mistress?'

'Well, if you like to put it that way. It might be as well to make sure. It's a big step. You want to be sure. You're going to hurt Beatrice like hell, so you want to be sure.'

'I am sure.'

'Sometimes these things wear off.'

'This is something different; I feel it is something I have been waiting for all my life.'

His remark was so corny that I couldn't help replying as I did :

'I'm told it is always like that.'

Bartels flushed. He did not reply.

I sat drearily watching the three bald men drinking cocktails across the room. They had dropped the masks now; they had got down to business, talking in low tones, heads thrust forward.

They looked solemn, keen, and avaricious, unaware that by my side a man who was gentle by nature, kindly and unselfish by instinct, was preparing an act of matrimonial treachery which was in contradiction to every fibre of his make-up.

When a man commits, or even seriously contemplates committing, an act which is not in tone with his character, he is in psychological trouble. Women are similarly affected, but to a lesser degree, because their characters are more flexible.

Bartels, that day at the Café Royal, was already in trouble. The beginnings were apparent to me as he sat breaking up the potato chips before him; breaking one up

45

and then prodding the bits around with his forefinger, and then breaking up another one, until in a short while there were no whole chips left in the little dish, but only a pile of very small broken morsels.

As I watched my friend, I hated the three big-paunched men.

At length Bartels spoke: 'The trouble is, you know, Beatrice has never been in love with me. Never. Not even at the beginning.'

'As wives go, that doesn't make her unique. Beatrice has got everything.' I went on, forgetting my resolution not to oppose him. 'Dammit, she's bloody attractive, efficient, witty, clever, and loyal. And fundamentally she's kind-hearted. She's a good girl, Barty. I don't know what more you want.'

Bartels turned, and looked at me for a few moments. His bright, intelligent, brown eyes had lost the enigmatic, sardonic look they often had. They were shining, with a curious, excited look in them.

'Well?' I said.

He took a deep breath. When he spoke, his voice, normally so strong and steady, had an undercurrent of nervousness about it which I had never heard before. It had the kind of tremor you hear when a diffident man gets up to make his first after-dinner speech.

'I always dreamed of a woman being really in love with me, Pete. I suppose it sounds silly to you. I've never told anyone before. At least, not till I told Lorna. Maybe it was because I got ragged a good deal at school. You remember how it was. I was a funny-looking youth. I suppose I dreamed about it the more, just because it seemed unlikely that any girl ever would fall in love with me. I suppose that sounds silly to you?'

'I don't know that it does,' I answered softly. 'No, I reckon I can understand that all right, Barty.'

I didn't look at him. I felt his eyes upon me, and knew that a wrong expression on my face, a wrong intonation in my voice, would shut him up. When a man is speaking to another man of love, of his inmost feelings, you've got to watch your step, almost hold your breath and cross your fingers, or he'll shy off like a startled horse.

'I proposed to her one day by a stream. It was a May day, very warm and sunny. We sat on a log, throwing twigs into the stream, and then I asked her to marry me. She hesitated for a while, then she said she would. So I kissed her.'

Bartels smiled. 'It was funny, that engagement kiss. She didn't kiss me; she let me kiss her. I think that even then I knew I was making a mistake. But I wouldn't admit it to myself. I thought I could force her to fall in love with me. Well, I couldn't.'

He had got over his nervousness now, and was talking quite fluently and easily.

'I wouldn't have thought Beatrice was cold,' I said. 'That's the last thing I would have thought.'

'She isn't. She's very passionate. I found that out even before we were married, though we never slept together. Once she had committed herself, she came to life, but physically only. Only physically, Pete. That's the point.'

'Maybe she was in love with you, and you couldn't see it.'

Bartels shook his head. 'No, she wasn't,' He hesitated, then added: 'It was sex, that's all. You see, I remember her kiss when we drove away from the church after our wedding. It was like the engagement kiss. It was as though all her doubts had come back to her. That's because she married me with her head and not with her heart, and she was wondering if she had done the right thing.'

He laughed, as though ashamed of his revelations, and sat back on his seat.

It is strange to see the anatomy of a marriage slowly and unexpectedly displayed before your eyes. Some people may enjoy it, but I didn't. I did not feel actual embarrassment, but something rather different and difficult to describe. It was as though one were reluctantly watching the disrobing of an old woman's body, once rounded and beautiful, or so one thought, and now shrunken and withered.

Bartels glanced round the room. He said:

'I remember I once said to her, years ago now, and in joking tones: "I think you only married me because I was the best financial bet among your boy friends. I had a private income, prospect of a good position in a good firm, and you would live in London. Your local boy friends hadn't as much to offer as that, had they?" I had been wanting to say it for a long time, because I suppose I wanted to hear her deny it, but I hadn't dared to risk it. Then one day, apropos of nothing, I just kind of blurted it out.'

He smiled affectionately. 'Beatrice can never lie convincingly. She doesn't try. She's too honest, you know.'

I nodded. 'Too honest, and too strong, too fearless.'

'She replied: "Well, I was very fond of you, anyway. And anyway, I love you now." I think she does, too, in her own way. She's never been in love with me, but I think she loves me today more than when she married me.'

He paused. Then he said, in a funny tone of voice: 'I always remember the kind of sick feeling I had when I heard her words. But I just laughed, and we didn't talk about it any more.'

'Well, we've all got to put up with something in life.' My remark was futile and pointless, and I only said it to fill in the silence.

Bartels said slowly:

'She is like a beautiful piece of mosaic, you know. She's

48

about perfect, except for one thing. The centre-piece of the mosaic, the thing I dreamed about, that's not there.'

'She's given you everything she had to give. It's not her fault if she can't give you romantic love.' And because he said nothing, I made the same remark I had made before. I said: 'We've all got to put up with something in life. We can't have everything, Barty.'

He shook his head and remained silent. So I knew that Lorna Dickson, whoever she was, had won. She might be a cheap little painted doll, she might be a well-groomed woman of the world; whatever she was like, she had won, and Beatrice had lost.

I thought sadly how heavily the dice was loaded against the wife in any triangle of this kind.

The other woman knows that the battle is on. The wife doesn't. The other woman is on her best behaviour, trying to please, to charm, to flatter, and often, I suppose, to seduce.

The wife, knowing nothing, is behaving like a natural person does: sometimes pleasant and amusing, sometimes dull, critical, or irritable. And silently watching her is her husband, noting her faults, comparing her with the alleged paragon of all the virtues.

I heard Bartels make his point again.

'You see, Beatrice has never been *in love* with me. It's so different.'

I turned towards him to tell him to be his age, to cease acting like a sentimental youth who has just discovered that love rhymes with dove. But I did not get a chance to tell him that, neither then, nor later, nor ever.

I saw him stiffen slightly, and sit upright, while a look came into his eyes such as I have never seen before on a man's face, though I've seen quite a few fellows who were supposed to be in love.

I will not attempt to describe it, I will merely say that

his thin, unimpressive countenance, with its wide mouth and spectacles, was suffused by something nearly akin to beauty.

As he rose to his feet, one forgot his meagre build, or the stupid tuft of hair on the crown of his head, standing up in disarray. One forgot everything except the beauty which sprang from the inner emotion of the man. That emotion, it seemed to me, was devoid of lust, greed, or even self-pity.

It is understandable. Hate can render a beautiful face ugly. The love inside Philip Bartels made his ugly face almost beautiful.

So I knew, without him telling me, that Lorna Dickson had come into the cocktail lounge. I wasn't expecting her, I was even startled and disconcerted, but I knew she had arrived.

Thus I met Lorna for the first time.

*

She was dressed, I remember, in a grey costume, but that is all that I do remember about how she was dressed. I was too fascinated by other things to take in much more.

I shall never forget the grace of her movements as she came towards us: the calm but friendly look in her steady, blue-grey eyes as she turned to be introduced to me: the mobility of her face when she smiled, which she did so often, and the laughter-wrinkles at the corner of her eyes.

She was not a pretty little painted doll; she was a mature woman of about thirty-three, gracious and charming, with light brown wavy fair, a slim figure, a small well-shaped head, and a jaw which was rather square, the mouth full but wide.

Above all, the impression I brought away from that lunch was of inner beauty matching that upon Bartels' face when he saw her come into the cocktail lounge. But whereas the beauty which suffused Bartels was sudden, called to life by the sight of Lorna, the beauty of Lorna, it seemed to me, resided perpetually within her.

Lorna! Dear, sweet, gentle Lorna.

You would willingly have lived out your life in loneliness rather than cause us suffering. That I know. You would gladly have stayed away from us had you known how things would develop.

But you couldn't know. In your innocence you came and lunched with us. Thereafter, not all your generosity, nor all your unselfishness, could stop the march of events.

It is all finished, the strain and the pain, the struggle and the tears. There is only peace, of a sort, for all of us. Peace, most of the time, but sometimes for me the agony of doubt concerning the crafty manner in which I afterwards acted towards my best friend.

*

It was over, by several months, when I revisited the château of our youth. It was finished, the climactic point reached and passed. Had I but remembered his words – 'Death is of no consequence – it is not dying that matters, it's how you die' – then it is possible, just possible, that I might have felt some inner warning, some hidden voice which cried: 'Stop! This woman is sacrosanct in the eyes of Philip Bartels.'

I might have acted differently, after that first meeting with Lorna Dickson. But I doubt it. I think I would have gone ahead just the same.

Such was my love for Lorna, born that day, that very day when she and Bartels and I had lunch together as friends.

Chapter 6

I KNOW so much now. I know, for instance, that on the day following the lunch at the Café Royal, Bartels went home in the evening with the firm intention of having things out, determined, despite what I'd said to him, to ask Beatrice to release him.

It was typical of his ingenuous nature, in so far as women were concerned, that although he dreaded the business he did not anticipate a prolonged fight. He thought she would be too proud, too strong, too independent to try for long to hold him.

He thought she would fight, with tooth and claw for a while, and then give in after a final burst of bitter invective, for she was a hot-tempered girl.

I thought she would fight with tooth and claw, but would not give in. She had too much to lose.

I thought he would have to leave her, and let time become his ally. I told him so, after Lorna had left us after lunch. He did not believe me.

The evening began in a normal enough way, Bartels and Beatrice watching a play on the television; and their dog Brutus dozing in front of the fire. He was a very old dog by now; an ugly, square dog, of mixed blood, with a white-and-tan coat, and a heavy head and jowl.

He had been given to them shortly after their marriage, and in those days he was a light and playful puppy; but now the weight of the years pressed heavily upon him; he was half-blind, and cumbersome, and lived only to eat and to sleep.

The television programme ended at about 10.15. The play had a strong love-theme running through it, and when it was over Beatrice went out and made some tea.

Bartels waited, biding his time until Beatrice should comment on the play. She poured out the tea and handed him his cup, and sat sipping her tea and looking into the fire. Five minutes passed, and he began to think that the opportunity for which he was waiting would not arise.

He sought in his mind for some method of approaching the subject. Now that the moment was near, he felt sad and nervous, as he always did at the thought of inflicting pain or distress.

Then, suddenly, Beatrice spoke about the play.

'I just don't believe in this grand passion, this all-devouring flame which people are always writing about,' she said irritably. 'It may occur in one case in a million, but I simply don't believe it holds true for the normal run of people, I just don't believe it.'

She sat in her arm-chair, stirring her tea, and looking into the fire.

It was her old line of argument, brought out and hacked around to all sorts and conditions of people; it was her attempt to justify to herself her actions in having married without being in love; an attempt to reassure herself that other people, or the vast majority, also married with their heads rather than their hearts, as she had done, as she would do again if she were widowed; that other people, therefore, had no fuller an emotional life than she had.

But that evening she seemed not to be content to let the matter stand. She seemed to be seeking an assurance from Bartels himself that she was right.

She said hopefully:

'Don't you think I'm right, Barty? Don't you think it's true that people see this love-stuff through a kind of rosy mist of self-deception?'

Bartels took a deep breath. 'No, I don't,' he said flatly. 'I believe in love.'

Beatrice reached to take a cigarette from a small table at

53

her side. The lamp-light fell on her red hair and fair complexion. She looked young and soft and, because she spoke in a low voice, somehow defenceless. But Bartels, hardening his heart, said:

'You think as you do, because you have not met the right man, yet.'

'Perhaps I'm not made like other women,' she replied hopelessly. 'I don't know. I can't feel this great overwhelming passion which people call love. I just can't feel it about any man.'

Bartels said again, dully: 'That's because you have not met the right man. If you met the right man you would feel it.'

But she shook her head. 'I can't give the adulation, the worship, the adoration, because I don't feel it. It's not in me to give it to any man. I can't help it. That's the way I am. I can feel physical passion, affection, comradeship, but that's all.'

'When you are in love,' said Bartels, 'you want to give, to protect, and to cherish too. But above all you want to give.'

'That, to me, is a form of magic in which I don't believe.'

Bartels said: 'Magic? Yes, it's magic all right. A formation of the eyes, a half-smile, the carriage of the head, each of these things can bring about love. It's magic all right. But a common enough type.'

'To me love means one thing.'

'What is that?'

'Sex.'

'Bed?'

'Bed,' said Beatrice. 'All the rest of it, the romantic dreams, the self-deception, what you call the wish to give and give, it all boils down to that. Bed. Love means bed. The rest is comradeship.'

Even Bartels had never before heard her express such a

disillusioning opinion. He was shocked and amazed. He shook his head.

'You're wrong,' he said, gently. 'You're utterly wrong.'

He felt an urgent wish to convince her that she was on the wrong track. It astonished and dismayed him that she should persist in this way of thinking.

Suddenly, unpredictable as she so often was, she said:

'But I do love you, in my own way. I do, really.'

'Do you?' He smiled affectionately at her. 'Perhaps you do.'

'Only I can't think anybody wonderful, because I try to see people with what I believe are the eyes of truth.'

'Why?' asked Bartels quickly. 'Why force it on yourself? Why be so practical? Why not live with a little fantasy, if it helps?'

'I can't.'

'Why not?' persisted Bartels. 'Why can't you?'

'Perhaps because I believe that truth, reality, is the most important thing in the world. It's not easy. It involves being truthful with yourself, and that's difficult. I try to be truthful with myself.'

'I think you succeed. Sometimes disastrously so.'

The little clock on the mantelpiece struck eleven, musically, harmoniously. Bartels felt cool and level-headed now, alert and vigilant, poised to strike the blow which he had planned. With a conscious effort he excluded any emotion from his mind, any pity from his heart.

He heard Beatrice say: 'You should have married a different woman, Barty. I love you, but it's not what you mean by love. You should have married a softer, more effeminate woman than me. The thing you need most, I can't give you. I try hard, but I can't. That's the tragedy of it. But I've given you everything I could. I've tried to be a good wife to you.'

'You've succeeded in being a good wife.'

55

Was there any harm in conceding that? he wondered. It was her just due. She had been an excellent housekeeper, a good lover; she had encouraged him in bad times. She had given him loyalty and comradeship.

For the second time that day he thought: she's like a fine mosaic, but for me the centre-piece is missing. It wouldn't have mattered for ninety-nine men out of a hundred, but it matters to me. It's her bad luck that I should be as I am. It's just her bad luck.

'I've not succeeded,' said Beatrice; 'I've failed. Perhaps not through my own fault, but I've failed because I have not given you what you want.'

Now, thought Bartels, shall I tell her now? For a moment the words rested heavily upon his tongue, but instead of speaking them he said:

'It is always risky for a woman whose heart is ruled by her head to marry a man whose head is ruled by his heart. I am as much, or as little, to blame as you. It's just one of those things. You've done a lot for me,' he added.

'Have I?' asked Beatrice. 'I wonder.'

'But a woman who does a lot for a man can pay a heavy price.'

Beatrice looked up. 'Meaning what?'

Bartels reached forward and stroked the dog's head. 'Oh, it's all rather complicated. Let's skip it. Can I have another cup of tea, please?'

He knew there was a risk that she might agree to drop the subject, but, understanding her, he reckoned it was a remote one. She took his cup and filled it and said: 'What is the price she pays? Tell me.'

'Let's skip it,' he said again.

'No, tell me. Go on.' She handed him back his cup of tea, and looked at him expectantly.

'Well, I think a woman is often like a thrush with a snail. She hops along, sees a man, pauses, listens, considers, head on one side, and then dashes him out of his protective shell and swallows him.

'A woman will knock a man into some semblance of order, cajoling, pleading, using every ounce of her personality, until she has moulded him into the shape she thinks is good for him. Then she sits back to enjoy the fruits of her labours. But she forgets the price she has had to pay: the blanketing out of his personality, the smothering process which had to be gone through.

'If he falls for another woman, she is surprised and hurt.

'She sees him as he was, and she sees him as she made him, a better finished product altogether. A product which another woman is now going to enjoy. I will agree with you that it is very trying for her.'

Beatrice sat with her hands folded in her lap, looking down at them, saying nothing. Bartels thought she was summoning her thoughts for a counter-attack, a final showdown. This was what he was prepared for. This was what he hoped for. Instead, she spoke quite quietly.

'You're a sentimentalist and a romantic, and I'm not. You should have married somebody else. I know you don't love me any more. You're terribly fond of me, you need me, you can't do without me, but you don't love me. Not any more.'

Now was the moment.

But he couldn't do it. He couldn't say the words because, with a sinking heart, he saw that she was crying; sitting bolt upright on the settee in front of the fire, holding her handkerchief to her nose; her face puckered up like a child's, mouth quivering to restrain her weeping.

'I'm too strong a character to suit you,' whispered Beatrice. 'I know I'm crying now, but I'm too strong a character. You should have married somebody weaker. You are the type which loves a helpless sort of woman. It's true, darling.'

Bartels thought: you can't tell with people, you just can't tell. She thinks she's strong, but at heart she's a child, wanting to be loved, and wanting to have somebody to love. Maybe everybody has three character-skins. The first skin is the one they try to present to the world, the deceptive skin; then comes the second skin, the concealed selfishness, the cynicism, the callousness, covetousness, and greed; but then, if you dig deep enough, right down below it all, you find the third skin, that of the essential, basic child, insecure, needing to be loved and to love.

You can't tell with people, you can't tell, he thought miserably.

'It's true, darling.' said Beatrice again, in a choked voice, 'you don't love me. You're terribly fond of me, I know. And I know you need me,' she said again. 'I know you can't do without me.'

A little wave of pity approached the barriers Bartels had erected around his heart. He saw it coming, and watched its approach with agitation, and raised the barriers higher against it.

She should never have married him, if she didn't love him. It was not fair. Or if she married him, she should have been prepared to give and give. He would leave her. He had to leave her, because Lorna was lonely, and needed him, and he needed Lorna. Fundamentally, it would serve Beatrice right.

She shouldn't have married me, he repeated to himself. She shouldn't have done it.

Beatrice suddenly buried her face in her hands. Her shoulders shook because she was weeping properly now. But there was little sound except for the periodic sharp intake of her breath.

She's fighting against it, thought Bartels irrelevantly, trying not to make too much of a scene. That's partly because she is English and partly because of her school train-

58

ing. It sticks, as Mr Chips said about Latin, some of it sticks. Blood and training. Some of it sticks; not all, but some.

The wave was lapping round the barriers now, eating at the foundations, lapping and receding, and coming back with renewed vigour. He only had to get up from his chair and take two steps, and sit beside her and take her in his arms, and tell her she was wrong, and she would believe him because she wanted to. It would all stop.

Beatrice said in a muffled voice: 'I only try to do my best, darling. It's not easy.'

Pity, pity, pity.

The fly in the wine-glass, the daddy-long-legs at the window, the butterfly in the fire. With dread and a feeling of foreboding Bartels saw the wave top the barrier and surge down upon him, and for a few seconds struggled against it with a hopeless ferocity. Then the waters were around him and over him, and he knew that he had lost. He rose from his chair and went over to the settee. He moved slowly and heavily.

I think that as he put his arms around her and told her that she was wrong, and that he did love her, there was already stirring within his mind, very faintly, and in an undefined form, the feeling that he might have to kill her.

*

It was the next day, 14 February, that, in accordance with his fortnightly habit, Bartels called upon his aunt Emily. Aunt Rose, pugnacious to the last, had died some years before, and uncle James, lost and at sea without that dominating character, had been buried beside her scarcely a year later.

But Cook was still in service, and greeted him in her usual sour manner, and told him that aunt Emily was at a seance but would be back in half an hour or so. He was hardly inside the door before he noticed a curious aromatic smell, half sweet, half acrid.

'What's that smell?' he asked.

'You may well ask,' replied Cook ominously; she was a fat, pale woman, with dark hairs on her upper lip and a slight but disconcerting cast in one eye. She disappeared into the kitchen without further words.

She had been with Bartels' aunt for twenty-seven years, and there appeared no reason to believe that she would ever leave until his aunt died. There was a general understanding that his aunt would leave her what she called 'a little something' in her will. Bartels remembered how sometimes, in the gentle, arch way his aunt Emily had of speaking, she would say in Cook's presence, while he was still a boy:

'There! What a lovely cake old Cookie has made for you to take back to school! What should we do without her? Never mind, Cookie knows she will not be forgotten when I pass over!'

She would glance at Cook, and give one of her coy little laughs, as if to indicate that she and Cook had a little secret which they shared between them. Possibly Cook saw visions of inheriting large sums of money, and retiring to live in modest comfort. Perhaps she thought she might even get the house. If she did, she was a stupid woman.

It was not that his aunt was mean, or even ungrateful for services rendered. It was simply that she had an entirely erroneous idea of the current value of money; when it came to tips she continued to think in terms of Victorian days. Quite often she would describe the details of some journey she had made; how she had caught this or that train; how she had arrived at Paddington and commissioned a porter to carry her bag for her; how they had found a taxi.

'So I gave the porter tuppence for himself,' she would say in passing, and no doubt she thought she had remunerated him very handsomely indeed.

Bartels went into the drawing-room and glanced at the evening paper for a while, and smoked a cigarette. There was nothing in the paper of particular interest. He tossed it aside and glanced round the room; then got to his feet and strolled over to the glass-fronted bookcase in which aunt Emily still kept the books of her late husband.

Bartels had only the dimmest recollections of his uncle Robert. He recalled a sombrely dressed figure who came and went with a mysterious black bag, who sometimes, when Bartels was a very small child, had come and gazed at him and made him put his tongue out, or had placed a glass thing in his mouth – 'a cigarette', uncle Robert had called it, with a wink at his mother.

Then the years passed and he never came again, and Bartels learnt that the physician had been unable to cure himself.

The bottom two shelves were filled with a collection of novels ranging from best sellers of pre-1914 vintage to Edgar Wallace and P. G. Wodehouse. The other two shelves held a number of fat medical works of reference, one or two volumes on the history of medicine, and a French and a German dictionary.

Sandwiched between the dictionaries was a red book called *Forensic Medicine and Toxicology*.

Bartels opened the bookcase and took it out.

The mentality of the poisoner was one which Bartels had never been able to fathom. He and I had frequently argued about capital punishment. Bartels was against it, except in very rare cases, declaring that in most cases the victim of a murder crime did not know that he was about to die, whereas capital punishment involved an almost sadistically long period of waiting and of fear.

'But poisoners,' Bartels said to me once, 'they're different. I just can't get inside the mind of a man who poisons his wife, for example. Imagine the mentality of a person who sees his wife waking up in the morning, and hears her say, "I think I feel a little better today," who sees her looking brighter and more hopeful, and then slips out and puts more of the stuff in her drink.'

Doubtless it was only morbid fascination that made him take the book out of the case, and sit down with it, and glance through some of the pages.

He noted some of the more common poisons, and their reactions.

Hydrochloric Acid, or spirits of salts, is a corrosive. The symptoms resemble, but are not so severe as, those produced by sulphuric acid. The smallest quantity that has proved fatal is one teaspoonful. In two cases, both young girls, this was sufficient to cause death. Recovery has, however, taken place after an ounce and half of the commercial acid has been taken, calcined magnesia having been administered ten minutes after it was swallowed. Death has occurred in two hours; the usual period is from eighteen to thirty hours. . . .

Oxalic Acid. When swallowed in poisonous doses, oxalic acid produces local effects which resemble those produced by the mineral acids; but unlike them, it exercises a special influence on the nervous system and upon the action of the heart. The smallest recorded fatal dose is 60 grains, which taken in the solid form caused the death of a boy aged sixteen. Recovery has occurred after an ounce and a quarter. Death has occurred in ten minutes, but it may be delayed for several days. . . .

Barium Chloride has been taken in mistake for Epsom salts. It has been taken for suicidal purposes in the form of rat poison, into the composition of some varieties of which it enters. . . .

Acute Arsenical Poisoning. . . .

Idly, Bartels turned over the pages. It seemed heavy and dull. He replaced it on the shelf. Next to it, he noticed a smaller, blue book, called *Toxicology: A Handbook for G.P.s.* He sat down with it.

Perhaps the fact that he had seen altrapeine among the bottles in the photographic darkroom in my flat caused him to pause and read about it.

Altrapeine, he read, was a synthetic poison with a cyanide basis . . . 'it is a white powder, odourless and tasteless, and easily soluble in water. It exercises a specially fast and usually fatal influence on the action of the heart. The circumstances of death are to all intents and purposes similar to those associated with coronary thrombosis. There is little or no pain. Death occurs within a matter of seconds, and in the case of a woman of forty it took place after a dose of a quarter of a teaspoonful. This poison is exceptionally difficult to detect.'

Bartels laid down the book and gazed across the room. He remembered Dr Anderson once saying that coronary thrombosis was the most merciful death of all. That was when Beatrice had had severe pains in the left breast, and had half seriously, half jokingly, suggested that she might have angina pectoris.

Dr Anderson had told him, in private, that the pain had been caused by Beatrice getting into an emotional condition. He had never discovered the cause of the emotional condition, and had soon forgotten all about it.

Dr Anderson had said something else, chatting to him in the way doctors do. He had said that coronary thrombosis could cause angina pectoris.

If, therefore, Beatrice – What? He stopped the train of thought. But it crept back, stealthily, and he followed it to its conclusion. If Beatrice died very suddenly, in circumstances suggesting coronary thrombosis, Dr Anderson would remember the earlier suggestions of angina pectoris. . . . It would confirm a diagnosis of coronary thrombosis.

He read the paragraphs again, and frowned.

A few moment later he heard his aunt's footsteps, descending the linoleum-covered stairs leading to the basement. After the death of aunt Rose and uncle James, she had redecorated the ground-floor rooms and let them, and now confined herself entirely to the basement.

Bartels rose quickly out of his chair, crossed the room, and replaced the book between the dictionaries. Perhaps it was this action, this quick, furtive movement, which first brought him face to face with the reality behind his thoughts.

But as he hastily picked up the evening paper again, and pretended to be reading it, his mind was still protesting against the evidence of his actions.

Now aunt Emily came into the drawing-room and gave one of her glad cries of welcome. She welcomed him in exactly the same way as on all such occasions. She raised her hands in pretended surprise, managed to infuse a delighted look into her eyes, and implanting a wet kiss on both his cheeks, said:

'My! My! My! If it isn't Phil? Well! Well! Well!'

Her good-natured oval face was wreathed in smiles. She gazed at him with every semblance of rapt attention. He knew that in two or three minutes she would be indulging in confidential remarks about the movements up or down of the Stock Exchange, for she prided herself on being a keen business woman, and the shortcomings of whoever at that particular moment happened to be occupying the top parts of the house.

But this time there was another topic. It was Chan, the Chinaman.

When Bartels asked her what the strange smell in the house was, she gave one of her mysterious little smiles. He knew those little smiles. They indicated that she was about to impart a confidential tit-bit of information. She said nothing for the moment, however.

For a while she sat by the fire, smiling mysteriously, and washing her hands with invisible soap. At length she said:

'Now if I tell you, you mustn't laugh. Chan wouldn't like that. I know what you are, you naughty boy.'

'I won't laugh,' Bartels said, and thought: Why did I get up so quickly and put the book back? Why?

'Promise?'

'I promise.'

She leant forward and gazed into his face.

'A wonderful thing has happened,' she said. 'I am being helped!'

'Helped? Who by?'

'By Chan.'

'Who's he?'

'Chan is a mandarin. He is a very, very important mandarin who was a high official at the Emperor's Court in Peking. He tells me that the Emperor did nothing, nothing at all, without his advice. He had to sit all day long at the Emperor's right hand and advise him on all the legal and financial matters which the Emperor had to decide.'

Bartels looked at her in surprise. He said:

'But how old is he? They haven't had an Emperor in China for ages.'

Aunt Emily smiled tolerantly at him, as though he were naturally too inexperienced to understand these things. She said:

'Chan has been *sent*, dear. There is no *age* where he is.'

'You mean he is a spook, or something?'

'He is my guardian spirit, dear. Oh! What a wonderful man he is! He is just the man I wanted, a legal and financial expert; just think of that, dear! I have had the most wonderful help from him. If I told you some of the things he has said, they would surprise you. You would really never believe it all!'

Bartels nodded. He knew it was no good arguing on this subject. He stared at her through his old-fashioned spectacles, and said:

'How did he get in touch with you?'

'It happened in the most wonderful way,' she said in a

low voice. 'It was little short of a miracle! I was at the greengrocer's ordering some vegetables when I saw quite an ordinary little woman standing by me looking at me in rather a strange way.'

Bartels said :'Had you ever seen her before?'

'Never. Now where was I? Oh, yes. Well, you know, she was staring at me in such a strange way that at first I thought she was rather rude. Then, just as I was leaving the shop, I felt a hand on my shoulder. I turned round and there she was again, and she said, "Excuse me, I'm afraid you must think me awfully rude, but I believe I can help you." I said, "Really, in what way?"

'So she led me to one side and said she had noticed I was carrying the *Psychic Weekly*. And only the previous evening her Guide had come to her and told her to watch out for me! He had given her, she said, an exact description not only of me but of the very clothes I was wearing! Right down to these long black ear-rings! Isn't that wonderful?

'She said her name was Mrs Brewer, and that if I would care to come that afternoon for a cup of tea she would get in touch with her Guide – a monk who was on earth in the fifteenth century, oh, such a wonderful man! – and she was sure that I would be helped.'

'So you went along?'

'So I went along. And Chan came through, too, dear. He said that from now onwards it was his work to help and advise me.'

'And has he?' Bartels asked.

'Has he indeed!' She clasped her hands together in the way she had when she was enjoying, or had just related, a joke of such richness as to be almost unbearable.

Bartels gathered that the long-deceased Oriental, while not binding himself to give detailed Stock Exchange tips, would point out that the market was rising or falling, that it was a time for courage or caution, and that although his protégée might have her times of bitter trial she would always win through in the end; because he would be by her side, talking through his good friend Mrs Brewer.

Hence the smell in the house, which was caused by joss-sticks, and was aunt Emily's way of showing her appreciation. She said Chan liked them, and she was luckily able to buy them from Mrs Brewer.

'Does she charge anything when you go there?'

Aunt Emily looked at him with an expression of joy and wonder on her gentle, placid face.

'Nothing! Nothing at all! She says that it is her mission in this world to help others to help themselves. She says she feels it would be wrong to accept money for this sort of thing. Mind you, I usually slip a few shillings into her hand when I go, just to help to pay for the tea, and she is more than satisfied. In fact, at first she didn't want to take it. I had to press it on her.'

Aunt Emily suddenly clasped her hands together again ecstatically.

'Oh, how silly I am! I haven't told you the most wonderful part! Chan says – just fancy! – that I should look carefully into the financial affairs, in boyhood, of poor uncle Basil!

'He says I must pay particular attention to the will left by his grandfather. He says everything is not all that it seems to be! Fancy! Do you know, dear, I have always had a funny sort of feeling – mind you, I'm not as psychic as poor aunt Rose was – but I have always had a funny sort of feeling that old uncle Basil should have inherited far more money than he did when his mother died.'

'You don't mean you are starting a case, too?'

But she was not to be drawn. She just smiled mysteriously, and said: 'Ah-ha! Wait and see! Perhaps you'll be surprised one day. Your old auntie Emily may surprise everybody yet!'

Bartels heard her voice droning on, and suddenly and ferociously wondered why he bothered to come to see her.

There was no emotional contact between the two of them, and never had been since the time when, a lonely and bewildered boy, he had first gone to live in the house.

They had treated him kindly enough, with the vague, detached benevolence of people who were eternally preoccupied with their own affairs. But that was all, and the emotions had coiled up tighter and tighter inside him, and even Beatrice had not held the key to the spring.

But you couldn't just not come any more, even though she was old and eccentric; indeed, you had to come just because she was that; so you went on calling once a fortnight, and you listened to her drooling on and on. You had no deep affection for her, and she had none for you, but you were a part of the routine of her life, something real in a world which for her was gradually becoming ever more unreal.

The aunt Emilys of this world, he thought bitterly, never had any friends. They had at the best a few relatives, who tolerated them, or not, as the case might be. They moved, eccentric and untidy, towards the grave, and nobody cared two hoots.

If you were normal, you shrugged your shoulders and said it was their own fault, and the devil of it was that the normal people were right.

If you weren't normal, if you were tortured by compassion and afraid of your own thoughts, you came once a fortnight, and were bored and irritated, because it was easier to pay a visit rather than stay at home and reproach yourself for not visiting her.

He saw aunt Emily rise and go across and open her writing-desk, which stood in a corner of the drawing-room, and watched her come back with a pencil sketch about eight inches by six inches.

'That's Chan. Madame Clevistki did it,' said aunt Emily.

'Madame who?'

'Clevistki. Isn't it beautiful? What a dignified, wise old face, eh?'

'Who on earth is Madame Clevistki?'

'She is a White Russian, dear, a friend of Mrs Brewer's. She is really a princess, you know, but she does not use her title. Oh, my, she's so psychic! Directly I shook hands with her it was like an electric shock going right up my arm.'

'I see.'

'She lived at the time of Peter the Great. A wonderful, wonderful woman!'

'Do you mean she is dead, like Chan?'

'No, no, no, dear,' said his aunt Emily chidingly. 'I mean that in her former life she was at the Court of Peter the Great. She has a most wonderful studio in the Fulham Road, and all the most famous painters come to her for lessons, says Mrs Brewer. Of course, she drew Chan in a trance.'

'Oh, of course. What did she charge you?'

'Nothing dear, only the cost of her taxi to and from Fulham Road; seven and six, I think it was, in all; and that was only because she had to fit the trance in between painting lessons. She is like Mrs Brewer, she feels she has been put into this world to help others. She doesn't feel she would be acting right if she made money out of her great psychic powers.'

He watched his aunt replace the drawing in the bureau and wondered whether Chan, the talented mandarin, would stagger them all at the next seance. Would his voice, constricted within the vocal chords of Mrs Brewer, burst forth in high-pitched tones and cry: 'Watch Philip Bartels! He has a lean and hungry look. He thinks too much. Such men are dangerous.'

Or would the voice, struggling with the unaccustomed syllables, say: 'Altrapeine. This poison is exceptionally difficult to detect. Its action is swift and painless and in the case of a fatal dose the circumstances surrounding the death of the subject closely resemble those attendant upon coronary thrombosis.' That, more or less, was what the book had said.

Bartels didn't think Chan would be so practical.

Chapter 7

IT is one thing to murder in a speculative kind of way, but except for those who blunder into the crime, there comes a pause between the impersonal contemplation of the deed, and the realization that there is the remotest possibility of the deed being carried through.

Again, excepting sudden acts of violence, the mind needs time to become attuned to the idea; the social sense inherent in all of us is instinctively outraged and requires a period of softening-up; the odds for and against success have to be calculated; and courage must be summoned to risk capital punishment.

For a man of Philip Bartels' temperament and imagination there comes, later, a curious interlude. The emotions involved in taking the decision have subsided, the greater emotions involved in the crime still lie ahead. Between plan and final action the husband, in the case of a married couple, regards his wife with a strange detachment.

There is no longer hate, if there ever were hate, for he knows that the cause of the hatred will soon be removed.

There is no longer gnawing greed, if her money be the motive, for his financial cravings will soon be satiated. And if lust for another woman is the driving force, he is soothed by the thought that shortly his desires will be completely fulfilled.

He watches her, therefore, in a detached way; sees her going about her household chores, cleaning, making the beds; observes her quietly reading in the evening, or sewing and listening to the radio; hears her, too, making plans; what dress she will buy, whom she proposes to invite to tea, what film she intends to go and see.

All the while he is thinking: 'You won't be doing that work much longer; neither sewing, nor reading, nor carrying out your other plans: that mechanism which you call your body will soon be stilled.

71

'You will be dead and in your grave. Finished. You think you have your own little future, like other people, and you are filled with your own hopes and modest ambitions.

'You think that I am fond of you; you think you can trust me, or you would not remain under my roof; you think I would even protect you from danger.

'But you're wrong. I'm going to kill you.'

The mind of the normal wife-murderer must therefore be almost animal-like in its lack of sensitivity, or it must be twisted, perverted with a kind of cat-and-mouse sadism raging within it.

But Bartels was an exception.

So far from lacking sensitivity, he had too much; and so far from being sadistic, he was too kind.

I brooded over these contradictions that evening when I returned to the château. I could not as yet entirely resolve the problem. I could not see how a man of Bartels' temperament could fill the role of one who was either cloddishly insensitive or gloatingly feline.

But I was continually conscious of a sensation of discovery, for I felt instinctively that as the next part of the story unfolded in my mind, I should be groping still nearer to the solution of at least one part of the mystery. I had already sensed that pity, the inability to inflict pain, had played a part in Bartels' action. What I had not hitherto realized was the devastating effect which this had had on him.

Now I was beginning to get a clearer picture and, collating all that I knew, I suddenly saw that, queerly enough, it was Beatrice herself who made up Bartels' mind for him, not by any conscious deed, or quarrel, or hurtful words, but by a small, instinctive action in the early hours of the morning, while she lay in bed more than three parts asleep.

Chapter 8

BARTELS had driven down to Thatchley, and dined with Lorna. She had been very sweet to him that evening, because she knew his kindly nature, and knew also, therefore, that a struggle was going on in his mind, though she obviously had no idea of its exact nature.

He left her at about 11.30 p.m. and set out on the road home, and Beatrice's chances of life increased as he felt the car answering to his touch and listened to the hum of the engine.

Driving, the feeling of controlling a car, always increased his self-confidence, helped to smooth out his worries. At such moments he recaptured a belief that, given the right set of circumstances, he still could carry out his earlier plan, and that he and Beatrice would be able to go their own ways in peace, and perhaps even friendship.

Bartels drove at speed that night, but without effort; he was a fine driver. The weather was dark, but cold and dry, and there was only an occasional car on the road at that hour. For long stretches at a time the road was well studded with cats'-eyes, and the bends were gentle.

As he drove down the slope leading into Cobham, his headlamps picked up a fox slinking swiftly across the road, its belly close to the ground. He caught a glimpse of its pointed mask, and was surprised to come upon a fox in that area.

For a few moments it distracted his mind from the burden which was weighing it down. He thought of uncle James, and his wish for one day out fox-hunting before he died; and of an abortive fox-shoot which he himself had attended in Germany in 1947; and of his last close view of Germany, when he hurried from the Volkswagen, out of

73

the sleet and the biting wind, into bomb-battered, dingy Hannover Station.

The station was dirty from day and night use by thousands of men, women, and children, refugees from the east, business men in shabby suits clutching attaché cases, and women with mysterious bulging cloth carrier bags back from the country after bartering clothes, jewellery, anything, for food.

There were deep shadows, and a few weak electric-light bulbs, and draughts, and the strange musty smell formed by a mixture of German ration soap, German-grown tobacco, German perspiration: and always the raw, icy wind blowing eternally through the battered station.

Bartels dropped smoothly into Cobham, and followed the road as it curved through the village to the left, and thought: there you had it, in Hannover Station, the fruition of the dreams of revenge, the final triumphant blossoming of hatred's hopes, the chance to look, to listen, to smell, to gloat, and to say: 'Serve the swine right! They asked for it!'

In the main hall of the station, he remembered, a woman stood with a cheap pram in which a child lay, and two other children stood by her side. She had a round, yellow face, and wore glasses and was tall, and not very fat or very thin: just dull looking. The group stood isolated beneath a light, caught in an island of illumination, as though picked out by an overhead searchlight, and the woman turned her head this way and that, as though looking for something or somebody, miserable and bewildered. That was defeat, that was our revenge.

If you went down below the station, to the former air-raid shelters, you found a thousand or two people herded together; some were there because it was warm, and the trains were always hours late, and you had to wait somewhere; others were there to do black-market deals; others because, in all Hannover, by day and by night, they had no other roof under which to shelter.

Here you met it again, hitting you in the face, the German smell, the stink of defeat and misery.

There were tables and hard chairs, but not enough, and a counter where you could queue and get a hot drink, if you had the right coupons. You picked your way carefully, in those foetid, smoky, musty vaults, shouldering your way through the human jungle, stepping over trunks, avoiding handbags, and legs, and feet, and bodies; some people were sitting or lying, some were awake, some sprawled asleep.

A seventy-year-old woman, with grey, streaky hair hanging lankly, sits on a suit-case, head on arms, knees up, eyes closed. A child lies across the end of a trunk, yellow hair touching the ground, sprawled out, ungainly, grotesque, as though a giant had used her as a toy, and then had tossed her down. She is asleep, despite the raucous songs from one corner of the room, the burble of voices, the shuffle of feet.

In the middle of the rooms the air is thick and foul and chokes you like cotton-wool; but it is warm, it is away from the vicious wind, and the sleet, and the snow. So you pick your way gingerly past the woman with the crying baby, and the filthy ragged man mumbling to himself, and past, with greater care, the groups of long-haired, grubby youths who hang about and plot and trade in cigarettes and other unobtainable things. They look at you curiously with their grey faces and grey eyes, and would like to provoke an incident and beat you up and rob you.

Bartels took the final bend in the road out of Cobham, and thought: it's so easy to hate at a distance. You read your newspaper, and you are well fed, and reasonably happy, and you say: 'Let 'em suffer. We did.'

But it's different when you've got to watch it.

75

You don't feel as you thought you would, when you see women with yellow faces trying to shield undernourished children from icy draughts on the slimy steps of a ruined station, and when you hear the desperate words with which despairing human beings have tried to comfort each other since the beginning of history.

That's what hurts, thought Bartels, the sight of people being unselfish in their miseries; trying to protect others, trying to cheer them when their own hearts are pools of unhappiness; trying to nurse them when there are no medicines, to give hope when there is none.

The man on the spot gets no satisfaction out of mass revenge; it is a thing to be read about and to be savoured from afar. The ordinary man has to stand at a distance to inflict suffering; if he comes too close he is lost. He becomes the victim of pity.

It is in man's nature to remove the cause of the pain, and if he cannot remove the cause, he will, as like as not, put the sufferer beyond the range of it. If he is a veterinary surgeon, he turns to the lethal chamber, and the sufferer sleeps. If he is a doctor, he may take equivalent action.

But for the suffering of the mind, of the broken heart which cries out in its agony of loneliness, the trusting heart which has been betrayed – for this kind of suffering, thought Bartels, there is no release.

There are mercy killings for the others, but none for these.

Nobody has ever reached out a hand to help them to sleep. And certainly nobody has ever killed to *prevent* such suffering.

'Or have they?' said Bartels aloud. 'Or have they?' he repeated, above the noise of the engine. 'You can't tell. You can't tell, because you can't see into people's hearts.'

By now he had reached the stage when he could coolly contemplate the use of altrapeine. The time when he had refused to face his thoughts, refused to understand why he did not wish his aunt Emily to see him with a book on poisons, that time was past now.

If I kill Beatrice, he thought bitterly, and if I am caught, I shall go down to history as a monster of callous cruelty. That's funny, of course, because if I did not care about her mental suffering, I could just walk out and leave her flat, and I wouldn't even risk my neck.

I could have all I want, without risk, without even great trouble, if I were the callous monster they will consider me if I kill and get caught.

'Yes,' said Bartels, aloud again, 'yes, it's funny, and it's silly.'

Outside Cobham, he saw a man walking by the side of the road. As he passed, the man turned and signalled for a lift. Bartels swore, and pulled up some yards farther down the road. He heard the sound of the man's feet pounding on the roadway as he ran to catch up with the car. Bartels opened the side door, and the man climbed in.

'How far are you going?' Bartels asked.

'Couple of miles farther on. Thanks for stopping, mate.'

The man was still breathless from running, but he began to fumble in his pocket, and pulled out a packet of cigarettes and opened it and offered one to Bartels: 'Have a "Wood", mate?'

'Thanks. You're out late.'

The man searched his pockets for matches, found one, and struck a light. He said nothing as he held the match for Bartels. Bartels glanced at him in the light of the flame. He was a middle-aged man, dingily dressed, with a thin, stringy tie, a cloth cap, and a lean, bony face.

Bartels wondered why he was out.

He thought idly that he might be a burglar, except that he hadn't a bag of tools; or a poacher, except that he wasn't wearing the kind of clothes you associate with a poacher; and he looked too old for a man returning from a love assignation.

'You're out late,' said Bartels again.

'I've been with my sister. My eldest sister.' The man drew on his cigarette.

'Whereabouts does she live?'

'She lived in Cobham. She died this evening.'

Burglar, poacher, lover, mourner, they all looked much the same. They all wore suits of clothes, and asked for lifts, and offered you cigarettes. Aloud Bartels said: 'I'm sorry to hear that. Very sorry indeed.'

The man drew on his cigarette again. Bartels saw the red glow in the windscreen. The man said:

'I was happy to see her go, and that's the bloody truth, mate. She's been hanging on for seven months. Well, we've all got to go some time.'

'That's right,' said Bartels, 'we've all got to go some time.'

'They didn't find out soon enough; that was the bloody trouble. You've got to catch it early with a growth; that's what the nurse said. A good nurse she was, too. It was a happy release, and that's the truth. A bloody happy release.'

Platitudes and clichés, one sneers at them, thought Bartels, but they have their uses. We've all got to go some time. A happy release. And all the others, ranged neatly in rows, potted and tinned and ready to hand for all occasions; the ever-ready solace and balm for simple folk, the soothing ointment for untutored minds. Aloud he said:

'Well, none of us can live for ever.'

'That's a bloody fact,' agreed the man. 'That's true enough.' He said nothing for a few moments, then he added: 'It was bad the last two days because the poison didn't burst the walls of her stomach, it kind of went to her brain instead; that's what the nurse said.'

Bartels felt slightly sick. Desperately he said: 'Yes, well, it's all over now. She's at peace now.'

He hoped the man had finished, but he had to have a last fling.

'They didn't find out early enough,' he repeated dully; 'that was Mildred's trouble. She was never one for running to bloody doctors. Not Mildred. There's a turning at the bottom of the hill, if you'd stop there, mate.'

Bartels stopped at the turning, and the man got out and thanked him, and trudged off down the lane. Bartels threw away the end of the Woodbine and drove on.

It was all over now, the man had said, and the man was right. If you didn't adopt that attitude about suffering, you went mad in the end. Suffering wasn't permanent, except in hell, if there was a hell; there was always peace in the end, one way or the other, and then the pain was finished, and the fear. Finished and over and at an end, for ever and ever; past, irrevocably past and done with.

That was the only way to cope with the suffering, the agony, and the fear in the world. Any other line of thought made you clutch your temples and groan aloud.

He drove through Esher and beyond, and turned right at the Kingston By-pass, and twenty-five minutes later crossed the Thames by Hammersmith Bridge. Hammersmith Broadway was deserted except for one policeman standing at a corner.

Bartels had a sudden desire to hear a strong, normal human voice unburdened by grief, untrammelled by worries, which would drag him from his own thought-world of speculation, and intrigue, and foreboding.

He stopped the car, and the policeman moved slowly over to him. Bartels lowered the nearside window, and the officer stooped down and looked through the window at him.

'Can I help you, sir?'

'Could you tell me the way to Alvington Road, please?'

'Yes, sir, it's near Olympia. Take the road facing you, and after the second set of traffic lights, take the first turning on the left, and you'll see it up on the right.'

'Thanks very much. It's a nice night,' Bartels added, reluctant to let him go.

'Lovely night. Bit cold out here, though.'

The policeman laughed good-naturedly. Bartels envied him. To Bartels the policeman represented sanity: a plain man, an honest man, leading a regular life, without fears for the future or regrets for the past. After the miserable conversation with the bereaved man, after the loneliness of the drive in the dark, Bartels clung eagerly to human warmth and said:

'All quiet round here, tonight?'

'Not a mouse stirring, sir.'

Bartels took out his cigarette case. 'Cigarette?'

The policeman hesitated, then removed a glove, looked briefly round the Broadway, and accepted one.

'Not supposed to, really, sir.'

'You'll probably find a quiet corner.'

'I wouldn't say it isn't done sometimes, sir. Thanks.' He smiled and put the cigarette into his breast pocket. There seemed little more to say.

Reluctantly, Bartels put the car into first gear and released the hand-brake. He bade the policeman good night and took the road leading to Kensington. His depression had lifted. He thought: I must get this thing into its right perspective. He would have liked to have had a drink with the policeman. Perhaps several drinks, so that they could reach the stage where personal problems could be aired, and the policeman would forget that he was a policeman and give the common-sense view of a down-to-earth man.

'Well, sir, if you're not happy with your wife, leave her,' the policeman would say in his solid way. 'There's no need to kill her. That's murder, sir, and there's no two ways about it. You get hanged for that sort of thing.'

'But it's to save her suffering and humiliation,' he would reply. 'What difference do a few years more or less make, in all the aeons of time which make up eternity?'

'I don't know what an aeon of time is, but I know what murder is.'

'It's a mercy murder; surely you see that?'

He imagined the man taking a gulp of his beer, and setting down his glass and saying: 'Murder is murder, sir, call it what you like.' And his own reply:

'But, dammit, she is flesh and blood, and filled with her hopes for the future. I am part of those hopes.'

Now he imagined the constable looking at him in surprise and heard him say:

'Don't think me rude, sir, but aren't you being a bit conceited? There are other men in the world, sir. She sounds a very attractive young lady. Anyway, there's no reason to kill her, sir, none at all. That's murder, that is.'

'You think she would get on all right without me?'

'I think she would be very hurt, sir. Especially in her vanity. Women are great ones for vanity, sir.'

'But she would get on all right in the end?' he heard himself insisting.

'I've no doubt she would get over it, sir. Anyway, she would rather take her chance, sir, if you were to be so bold as to put it to her.'

By the time he had reached the traffic lights at Holland Road he had made up his mind. He saw now that he had been overdramatizing things. He had been neurotic and hypersensitive and ridiculous, and had very nearly put his neck, literally, into a noose.

It was perfectly simple, after all.

He would leave Beatrice and go and live in digs again, near Lorna. He would do just that. He would give Beatrice a handsome share of his income. Five hundred a year, that's what he would give her. Tax free, too. A good income that, even in these days.

She would be all right on that. If he earned more money, he would give her a share of that, too. He'd be generous all right. She never would be able to reproach him on that score. Then she would divorce him, and he would be able to start afresh with Lorna. Just the two of them, together, for always.

Beatrice was a strong character really; she just had moments of weakness; but Lorna needed him and he needed Lorna. Beatrice would be hurt, which was a pity, but she wouldn't live in a wilderness of loneliness as Lorna would without him. Lorna wasn't as strong as Beatrice.

Beatrice would go out into the world again and, with her indomitable courage, carve out a new life for herself, probably a far better life than she had led with him. He felt queasy as he thought how, through a total misjudgement of the situation, he had so nearly placed himself within reach of the Law. After all, however clever you were, there was always a chance that you would be caught.

'There's always the risk,' he murmured, 'there's always the risk.'

By the time he had driven up to the door of his block of flats, he knew that what he had decided to do must be done quickly. He knew himself, at least to some extent.

In two days he was going up north again. In Manchester, he would write Beatrice a letter explaining things. He would praise her to the skies, and the praise would not be unmerited. He would take all the blame upon himself, blacken himself, castigate his own weakness.

There would be no criticisms, no reference to previous quarrels, no harking back to grievances and past disappointments, no suggestion at all that since she had married with her head rather than her heart she was at least partly to blame.

Then he would simply not come back.

Knowing himself, he knew that he might weaken if he came back, and if she cried and implored him to give the marriage another chance. He wouldn't risk it.

As it was late, he left the car in front of the house and went upstairs to the flat. He let himself in quietly, and switched on the light in the hall, and glanced casually at the letters on the hall table.

There was a Final Demand from the gas company, a document from the authorities telling him that unless he appealed he would be summoned for jury duty, and a bill from the local garage: a fairly representative selection of letters, in fact. He stuffed them in his overcoat pocket. Before he left, he would clear up all outstanding bills; he would leave her clear, able to make a clean statrt.

He made his way to the kitchen and cut himself a thick slice of bread and cheese, and ate margarine with the bread to economize the butter ration. Beatrice did not like margarine.

There was three-quarters of a pint of milk in the refrigerator. He poured himself out a cup, then realized that there would not be enough left for coffee for breakfast. Beatrice preferred coffee to tea. He poured the milk back into the bottle, and replaced it in the refrigerator, and quenched his thirst with water.

It made him feel like a man apologizing for stepping upon the toe of an individual into whose back he was shortly to plunge a stiletto.

Bartels went into the drawing-room, and stood by the embers of the fire which Beatrice had made up for him. He looked around the room, noting objects which linked him to the past.

There was the picture of the Seine which he and Beatrice

had bought in Paris while on their honeymoon, upon which, indeed, they had spent more money than they could afford. There was the set of porcelain horses Beatrice had bought while visiting a friend in Belgium. And the Victorian silver picture frame, holding a picture of Beatrice as a girl: the first thing they ever bought for their home.

He looked at these things, trying to resurrect from the ashes of his emotions some tiny flicker of sentiment. But there was nothing left; it was all dead, grey, unstirring, and without warmth. He saw only a painting, some china objects, and a frame with a good-looking girl in it.

He threw the remains of his cigarette into the grate and began to undress in the drawing-room, as he always did when he was late, in order not to disturb Beatrice. He went into the bedroom in his shirt and underpants, and quietly slipped them off and put on his pyjamas.

Beatrice had left the gas-fire burning, half turned up, and he turned it up higher and stood by it, warming his feet and hands.

By the light of the fire, he could make out the two twin beds, side by side. Beatrice was asleep, lying on her back, one arm above her head, as though she had found the room and the bed-clothes too hot. As his eyes grew accustomed to the dim light, he saw something white on the small table by his bedside, and moved silently across to see what it was.

It was a mince-pie. Under the mince-pie was an envelope addressed to him in Beatrice's handwriting. On the envelope she had written: 'Eat the pie, and read the letter.'

Bartels ate the pie. It was freshly made and crumbly. He knelt by the fire and opened the letter. The slight noise caused Beatrice to stir. She murmured his name sleepily.

'I'm back,' he replied softly.

She said something he could not catch, and turned over

84

on her side and fell asleep again. He opened out the letter and read:

Darling Barty,

The beginning of the year is the time for other new beginnings. I know I have often been other than that which you wanted in your heart, though you have never said so. But I have done my best for you, darling. I will try to be better still. You have made me very happy over the years, and I want you to know how I appreciate it. I've made some more pies. Hope you liked this one!

Your own Beatrice.

He folded the letter and put it back in its envelope, and placed the envelope on the mantelpiece. He thought: to-morrow evening I must go out. I can't stay at home. If I stay at home I shall weaken. I must make some kind of excuse. I must get out tomorrow evening.

He turned the fire out and climbed into bed, and drew the sheets up to his chin and lay staring into the darkness. All his movements had been slow and noiseless, but the slight creak of the bed disturbed Beatrice.

She thrust her hand through the bed-clothes, and out of her bed, and fumbled for Bartels' hand. She found, not his hand, but his forearm, which seemed to be sufficient, for she sighed, as if with content, and dropped off to sleep again.

Bartels lay still, rigid, as the old turmoil of fear and pain and confusion gripped his stomach, and spread up his body to his throat. Then the pain and the fears dispersed, and only the confusion remained, and withdrew to his brain whence it had originated, and remained there a while, circulating round and round and round.

He kept it there as long as he could, fighting against certainty, because so long as there was confusion there was no decision, and so long as there was no decision there was no action, and without action there was safety.

But the uncertainty dispersed, too, in the end, as he knew it would.

So that he had to face the truth. It was not as though she were awake and play-acting. She had been three parts asleep. It had been an instinctive, almost subconscious action. The movement of the hand, with its groping, fumbling action, had wiped out the memory of the imaginary argument with the police constable. It had removed all the comfortable hopes.

He was not even back where he was. It was worse. There was no escape now, no more reasons for delay, no excuses which the hand of Beatrice, reaching out for him in the darkness, had not placed far beyond his reach.

I do need you: that's what the hand had said. I may seem tough and self-reliant, and competent, but I'm not. I'm glad when you come back. I may not love you as you would like to be loved, but I need you. I'm glad when you return, because I don't like being left alone. Fundamentally, I'm unhappy and unsure when I'm alone. Always come back to me. I do my best, I can't do more, so don't ever leave me. I would be so lonely, so frightfully lonely inside me, and so cold.

Bartels stared up into the darkness, his wrist gripped by the hand of Beatrice, fighting the old hopeless forlorn fight against the waves of pity.

Once, he tried, with infinite care, to disengage himself, but Beatrice sensed his intentions through her sleep, and tightened her grip. So he continued to lie on his back, while the certainty of what he must do grew stronger in his mind.

Because it was a cold night, the hand which gripped his wrist grew cold as the hand of a dead woman, or the hand of a woman to whom death had now come very close, even though there were, in fact, some days to go before 26 February.

Chapter 9

Two days later, travelling by a very early train, Bartels went to Manchester, as he had planned. In the evening, he sat in the writing-room of his hotel. He felt cold, tired, and dispirited. The room was curiously named, because there were no pens, no writing-paper, no blotting-paper, and the ink-wells were dry. But there were a few shoddy desks, and if you asked, they would reluctantly give you a few cheap sheets of headed notepaper at the reception desk.

There was a smouldering fire in the grate, but in spite of the fire the room was chilly, and a raw wind hammered periodically at the windows.

Round the grate sat three other commercial travellers. Bartels, trying to compose a letter to Beatrice, was distracted by their conversation.

Two of the men were in their thirties, thin, sharp-featured, red-faced fellows. The third was about fifty, a pale-faced man with a bald head and signs of exophthalmic goitre. Their talk ranged from world politics and the atom bomb to the current trade position.

Later, one of the men dropped his voice and began to talk about somebody called Fred with whom the three had been drinking earlier.

Fred, it appeared, was unfaithful to his wife, and he was regarded with amused admiration by the three before the fire. They related the various excuses he made to his wife, and laughed at his astuteness. Fred was a bit of a dog.

Bartels wondered why they bothered to lower their voices, since every word was audible to him. He also wondered why they thought Fred was so clever.

Fred wasn't clever. Anyone with half a brain could deceive his wife, provided his wife was a normal, trusting individual. What was clever about pulling the wool over the eyes of somebody who trusted you? What's so frightfully bloody clever about that? thought Bartels irritably. Children can do it. Even dogs.

He felt like throwing down his pen and shouting: 'What do you oafs know about the inner subtleties of deception, of the deceiver who suffers more than the deceived? You clods! You sit here, crouched round the fire, smirking and leering, and what do you know of the pain of the imagination? You, who snigger like smutty-minded schoolboys, what right have you to gabble about infidelity?'

He pictured the look on their faces as they swung round at his words. Indignation as the insults, first, then a strained look as they tried to puzzle it all out, and then, of course, the reproaches:

'Excuse me, old man; but this happens to be a private conversation.'

'No need to be insulting, old man.'

'Who are you, anyway, to come butting in?'

He picked up his pen, and began to write, trying so to concentrate his thoughts as to exclude the talk around the fire.

Dearest Beatrice, he wrote, but above the rattle of the windowpanes, he heard the fat man's wheezy voice:

'So Fred says without a second's hesitation, "All right, dear," he says, "if you don't believe I stayed there, ring 'em up and ask 'em, write to 'em, do what you like, dear, if you don't believe me," and then the three pips goes and he cuts off with a quick good-bye. Of course, he knew she wouldn't have the nerve.'

A louder gust of wind rattled the windows and drowned the rest. Bartels gazed at the notepaper. *Dearest Beatrice.*

The lout Fred was a fool; otherwise his wife would not be suspicious. You can deceive your wife for years and years, thought Bartels drearily, if you're not a boorish, ham-fisted clot like Fred. There must have been a time when Fred's wife was as trusting as Beatrice.

Bartels sighed.

He crumpled the sheet of notepaper up because he had smudged it, and took another, and wrote a brief letter to Beatrice saying that he hoped to be back on the next day but one.

Then he went up the narrow, winding staircase to his room at the top of the hotel. The room was cheerless and sordid, a measure, he supposed, of his own lack of success as a wine salesman. He wondered why they couldn't take him off the road, give him a job in the office. He'd be all right in the office. He was no good on the road. Hadn't got the aggressiveness, the smooth talk, the self-confidence.

Sometimes he asked himself why they sent him out at all. Did they, too, suffer from pity, and talk behind his back, and say: 'Poor old Barty, he's no good, of course, but we can't sack him. Had a hard time, in the war, you know. Keeps our name before the buyers, but that's about all.'

He felt the blood mounting to his face as, for one moment, he wondered whether Lorna Dickson's feelings, also, were based upon pity He thrust the thought from him, and gazed round the room, noting despondently the mass-produced furniture, the linoleum-covered floor with the narrow strip of carpet by the bed, the window-panes of frosted glass so that you could not see out of them, and the one harsh electric-light bulb hanging from the middle of the ceiling.

There you had it all within four walls, the furnishings of failure, the symbols of the commercial traveller who was no good, who never had been any good, and who, despite all his efforts never would be any good.

He undressed in the freezing, unheated room and crawled into bed, and lay in the darkness. He thought of the lout Fred, who was so devoid of finesse that he was hard put to it to lull the suspicions of his wife, and he wondered what the wife was like. Did she sit by her fireside, alone, bitter, and in tears, the unwanted woman; or pace up and down, up and down, like the wife of the former District Commissioner used to do in the house in Melville Avenue?

He turned over on to his side. A chambermaid, with unexpected zeal, had placed a stone hot-water bottle in the bed. He pressed his feet harder against it to gather the warmth.

He thought that although she didn't realize it, Fred's wife had little to worry about. Fred would grow tired of his bits of stuff. Fred would always come home in the end. All the Freds in all the world would always come home in the end. But I'm different, he thought. For me there is no light-hearted dalliance; there never could be, because if you've got any imagination you can't just love 'em and leave 'em; not if they're sensitive, and if they're not sensitive you don't fall for them.

The warm air from the bottle and from his body, trapped within the bed-clothes, slowly surrounded him, soothing his nerves and lulling the agitation in his mind.

He was comfortable now, warm and comfortable, and had no wish to fall asleep. Instead, he wished to stay awake awhile with the image of Lorna before his mind's eye, to feel in imagination the softness of her lips and the silkiness of her shoulders beneath his hand.

But the day's events intruded. It had been a bad day, of course; there was nothing unusual about that. Buyers had been obstinate, some even refusing to see him. There ran through his mind the old time-honoured excuses which he had heard so often over the years:

'Mr Fowler asks if you will excuse him this time, as he is very busy.'

'Mr Roberts has the auditors with him and regrets he cannot see you.'

'Mr Martin is in the middle of stocktaking, and is sorry he cannot have the pleasure of seeing you on this occasion.'

'Very nice of you to call. Mr Andrews has asked me to say, however, that he is well satisfied with his present suppliers and sees no reason to change.'

The list of his wines ran through his head. Once he had thought them colourful and romantic. Even now they had a lilt about them, though, as he grew sleepier, the music was interrupted with snatches of his own sales talk, with thoughts of Lorna and Beatrice, and quantities and prices, and still more sales talk ... St Émilion, St Julien, Bordeaux Rouge; Médoc, Beaune, Pommard; Chambertin, Beau-Jolais Supérieur – 'we have a most interesting parcel of Beaujolais'.

A most interesting parcel of Beaujolais, and at a keen price, and just the thing for your clientele. A full-bodied wine for the North, and Lorna came from the North. . . . I love you, Lorna; I love you, Barty; I shall understand if it's too hard, Barty, I shall understand. . . . Bordeaux Rouge, Pommard, Médoc. . . . Lorna, darling Lorna, don't say that you, too, suffer from pity? . . . Lorna, my love. . . . Cut the commission. Five per cent on bulk wines. Two hogsheads, four hogsheads, eight hogsheads, and quarter bottles to contend with high restaurant prices.

Quarter bottles, a mixed case of eight quarter bottles, and pamphlets and a map for the Bordeaux wines. Of interest to customers, a help to the waiter! The trend to expect is a rise in Burgundies. . . . It's not what a man does, or even whether he succeeds, it's how he does it that counts.

said Lorna once. . . . Dear, sweet Lorna. . . . A narrow market, a narrow market, wine fifteen shillings, duty twenty-six shillings, three-and-six freight and insurance, ten shillings bottling, price in bin fifty-four-and-sixpence, and a most interesting parcel of Beaujolais.

One hundred gallons, forty-eight dozen, two hogsheads. Four hogsheads. Eight hogsheads. Something special in St Julien, St Émilion, Médoc, Beaune, Chambertin, Mâcon, and Bordeaux Rouge. . . . Don't ever leave me, that's what the hand of Beatrice had said to him in the dark. . . . I need you.

Bartels sighed, confused, more than half asleep.

Beaujolais . . . a most interesting parcel of Beaujolais. . . . A most interesting parcel of altrapeine. . . . Just in case. . . . I must buy a most interesting parcel of altrapeine. . . . Somehow. . . . Tomorrow. Without fail. Altrapeine . . . of interest to the customers, a help to the waiter. Bartels smirked once, drowsily, then slept.

*

Although Bartels fell asleep without too much trouble, he had a restless night disturbed by dreams. In one he was offering a sample of Beaujolais to a buyer, but he couldn't make the wine come out of the bottle because, try as he might, he was unable to tilt the bottle to the right angle; meanwhile the buyer waited, watching and sneering.

In another dream, Beatrice and Lorna alternately reproached him and wept, while the dog Brutus lifted his heavy brown-and-white head and looked at him mournfully and said, 'It can't be done, it can't be done, and well you know it, young man.'

And once he woke, sweating and trembling, and clutching the bed-clothes, his heart racing and thumping, from a dream in which he found himself locked in a cabin on a ship. When he rattled the handle and called for help, the voice of a man he knew to be Fred shouted through the ventilator: 'It's false, old man. It's not a handle at all, old man. We're at the bottom of the sea, so why worry, old man? If you don't believe me, ring me up, write to me, do what you like, old man.'

The chambermaid woke him at 7.45, in the half-dark, with a cup of lukewarm, red tea. He heard her set the cup of tea on the chair by his bedside and move towards the door. He raised himself on one elbow and said: 'May I have a bath-towel, please? They've only given me a hand-towel.'

The maid was a middle-aged woman with a lined face rendered discontented and querulous by too much work, too much stair-climbing, too much clearing up of other people's disgusting messes. She turned at the door and looked at him in surprise, and said in a flat Lancashire accent: 'Bath-towel? You don't get bath-towels in this hotel. Not in this hotel.' She went out.

Bartels gulped down the red, bitter tea, and lay back, trying to summon the energy to get out of bed into the cold air. But he was tired from his restless night, and his limbs ached. He closed his eyes, intending to rest for ten minutes. When he awoke, it was a quarter to nine.

He made his way to the bathroom at the end of the corridor, and opened the door. A man was sleeping on a camp bed near the bath. He returned to his bedroom. At 9.30 he went down to the dining-room, and sat at a table by himself. There were marmalade stains and toast-crumbs on the cloth.

'Good morning,' he said to the waitress. 'What's for breakfast?' He tried to sound cheerful. He was sorry for waitresses in seedy hotels. She replied:

'Breakfast? You'll be lucky if you get a cup of tea and a slice of toast. Breakfast finishes at 9.30.'

'Well, it's only just 9.30,' he replied wearily.

'It's two minutes past.'

He looked at the clock. She followed his glance, and said: 'That clock's slow. Staff breakfast time is between 9.30 and 10; that's the trouble, see? Besides, we don't get paid between 9.30 and 10. I'm willing to serve the stuff, but the chef, he won't have it, see? That's the trouble.' She paused and smiled grimly. 'When I first came here, I was ashamed to face the customers; now I'm as bad as the rest.'

Bartels said: 'Bring me what you can, then. It can't be helped.'

Surprisingly, having gained her point, she took his order without further fuss.

It was a shocking breakfast. He asked for tea and cereal, and he was brought coffee and porridge. This was followed by a piece of shrivelled smoked haddock. Instead of sugar for the porridge, there was watered-down syrup in a jug. Sugar for the coffee consisted of two tiny cubes, and there were two thin wafers of margarine for the toast.

In the middle of eating his porridge, Bartels heard a man shout plaintively across the dining-room: 'Can't I 'ave my 'addock, Miss?'

Five years after the war, thought Bartels, and no breakfast after 9.30 except on sufferance. He picked disconsolately at his fish, and thought of his uncle James, in his loud check suits, his jaunty brown bowler hat and white socks.

Uncle James would have raised hell. He would have stormed and banged and called for the manager, and sent the coffee back; and had sugar for his porridge and butter, and lots of it, for his toast.

Finally, he would in all probability have got away from the hotel without paying his bill, and even, with the help of the genius of aunt Rose, have borrowed a fiver off the manager – to be paid back, tenfold, of course, when the great case was won.

But they were proper salesmen, and I am not, thought Bartels, I am just a bum commercial traveller who is now going to sneak out and buy some poison, if I've got the guts.

*

Bartels had no difficulty at all in buying a two-ounce bottle of altrapeine. The only mistake he made, and, as it turned out, it hardly mattered, was in trying to be a little too clever.

On the way out of the hotel he stopped by the letter-rack and examined some of the letters. What he wanted was a genuine name and address which was easy to remember. One of the letters was addressed to: A. Thompson, Esq., 99, Rugely Avenue, Bradford. He thought that would do very well. That would look as well as any other name in a poison-book.

The chemist shop he decided to patronize was a large one in the middle of the city. He stood outside it a moment, watching the people enter and leave. Then he went in, and made his purchase.

He thought the assistant might ask him what he wanted such a dangerous drug for, but he didn't. It was absurdly easy, thought Bartels, as he handed over the money, and took out his pen to sign the dangerous drugs book.

It was then that he made a slight slip, owing to the fact that, to make himself less easily recognizable should anything ever go wrong, he had removed his spectacles before entering the shop.

He tried to sign his name in the wrong column.

It gave him a bit of a shock, of course, because the assistant laughed as he corrected him and Bartels did not wish to attract attention, either by causing laughter or in any other way.

Later that day, he turned his car towards London. Once

or twice he put his hand into his overcoat pocket to make sure the bottle was really there, that the whole thing was not a dream. His mind was not yet one hundred per cent attuned to murder. But it was by the time he reached London.

Chapter 10

WHILE Bartels was fumbling towards his crisis, I was making my own plans. I was crafty all right. I've already admitted as much. I wanted Lorna Dickson, and I made the necessary plans to get her. It is odd that I, Peter Harding, the cosmopolitan, the hotel proprietor, the cynic, had fallen for the woman at one meeting.

Yet that is one of the effects which Lorna Dickson had on people: either she made no impression at all, or else, once you had met her, you could think of little else.

I do not know why I fell in love with her. She was no longer a young girl. She had no classic beauty. She was not even unusually witty. So much my brain told me. My senses told me that she was the only woman I had ever met whom I seriously wished to marry. It was all illogical and even nonsensical, but it was a fact.

Lorna occupied my thoughts by day and by night, so that sometimes I hardly paid sufficient attention to the business at the office; instead, I would sit dreaming of her, of a future with her, or torturing myself with the thought that I might lose her to Bartels. The latter, however, was a mere masochistic game; given time, I knew I could beat Bartels.

But first I had to persuade myself that though it might cost me the friendship of Bartels, I had right, of a sort, on my side. For that is the hypocritical way some are made, and I am one of them.

Since I was determined to be so convinced, it was easy. It was merely a question of selecting the most telling argument. I pointed out to myself that I was unmarried, and Bartels was married, and married, too, to a jolly good wife, in whom any ordinary man would rejoice. Further, Beatrice did not deserve a blow of this kind.

I dismissed all Bartels' own arguments as specious and finicky. I was pretty well off, too, one way and another, whereas Bartels, to put it frankly, was a bit of a failure. He was unlikely ever to have enough money to pay his wife an allowance and to keep Lorna in any real comfort. In fact, Lorna would probably have to continue with her dress-making if they were going to do anything more than barely make ends meet. It was an iron-clad alibi for an act of treachery to a friend.

I always remember how innocently I wheedled her exact address and telephone number out of Bartels. It was the day the three of us had lunch together, and afterwards, when Lorna had gone, I said to him, quite casually:

'Where abouts does she live, Barty?'

'Outside Woking,' he replied. 'Near a village called Thatchley. She's got a small, Georgian-style house. Runs a small car, and has quite a nice little business in the neighbourhood.'

'Thatchley,' I said thoughtfully, as though I had heard the name somewhere before. 'Thatchley. Yes, I remember now, I've seen signposts pointing to it on the road to our hotel near Guildford.'

His face lit up, as though the mere fact that I had seen a signpost pointing to her village was a source of pleasure to him. Poor, foolish old Bartels. It was all so damned easy.

'Yes, I know now,' I said lightly. 'Yes, of course – Thatchley, near Woking.'

I remember we had fetched our hats and coats, and were standing in the vestibule before parting. He said:

'If you pass that way during a week-end, pop in and see her. She gets a bit lonely during the week-ends. It's not so bad during the week, because she is often seeing people.'

Easy, dead easy, it was.

'She won't want to see *me*,' I said deprecatingly, for I intended to cover my tracks.

Bartels took the bait with one gulp. 'She will,' he said eagerly. 'I assure you, she'd love to see you.'

'Oh, I don't think so,' I replied. 'Not me. I don't think she wants to see me.'

He was like the lemmings of Norway, which rush down to the coast and swim out to sea and drown. He just plunged on to his fate, because he thought he could trust me and because he knew that Lorna was lonely at weekends.

'She likes you,' he insisted.

'How do you know?'

'I could see. I can always tell when Lorna likes somebody.'

I hesitated deliberately. 'Oh, well,' I said, 'perhaps one of these days I'll call in. I'll see.'

So he gave me Lorna Dickson's address. More, he gave me exact details of how to find her house. He said he wanted to make absolutely sure that I would find it all right. Fool.

My attitude towards Bartels is changing as I write the record. I know that. It is changing as it changed that day when I revisited the château and re-lived this story.

I was always tougher than Bartels. More efficient. More worldly and realistic. Bartels was a dreamer, I am not. It is no good being a dreamer if you are running hotels. Perhaps that is why he liked me and respected me.

So I always start off by thinking of the Bartels of my youth with nostalgic affection. But as this story progresses, as I see how I fooled him and beat him, all along the line, I begin to lose patience with him. I know – indeed, I insist – that despite everything he was a gentle-hearted and kindly fellow. And I pity him, but in a contemptuous kind of way. This I regret, but cannot help.

*

Just beyond Cobham there is a fork in the road; the left branch carries on to Guildford, the right one leads to Byfleet and Woking. You have to take the Woking road, and follow it for some time before you come to the lane in which Lorna Dickson's house was situated. It was while Bartels was in Manchester that I visited her first.

I found the house quite easily, thanks to Bartels' instructions, despite the darkness and some falling sleet.

It lay behind a thick yew hedge considerably older than the house, so that I was not surprised to learn later that the modern house had been built upon the site of a couple of early Victorian labourers' cottages.

A wrought-iron gate opened on to a stone-flagged path which led past a flower-bed and small lawn to the white front door. Two apple trees stood in front of the house, and the house itself, built of light red brick, was pleasant enough with its clean, straight lines, and large windows. It was not large, having, as I learnt later, a drawing-room, dining-room, workroom, and kitchen downstairs, and, upstairs, three bedrooms and a bathroom.

I had telephoned her and told her I would like to call in at about 6 p.m. on my way back to London from Winchester. She must have heard my car draw up in the lane, for she had opened the front door, and switched on the porch light, by the time I had passed through the wrought-iron gate.

So I saw her for the second time: standing in the doorway, slim, of medium height, small boned; dressed in a black barathea coat and skirt, and a turquoise-blue blouse. The light fell on her wavy, light brown hair, and, when she shook hands with me and looked me in the face, I thought once again that she had the most attractive eyes I had ever seen. It occurred to me, too, that her face combined, in a most unusual manner, well-defined features with undoubted prettiness. The two do not normally go together. It was a face which would wear well, through the years; a face which would look handsome in middle age and even old age.

Glancing over what I have written, I see that I have completely failed to describe the charm of Lorna Dickson. I have used the word handsome, yet to me, when that word is applied to a woman, it conjures up somebody rather Juno-esque and forbidding. Lorna was not at all forbidding. Again, I have said that her eyes were attractive, and that might somehow imply a certain superficiality, or lack of intelligence: but Lorna, as I soon discovered, was a very intelligent woman.

I followed her into the house, and into the drawing-room. This was a pleasantly proportioned room, in which modern decorations had been combined with antique furniture and with comfort: for one thing, there were a couple of deep armchairs, and a large, chintz-covered settee in front of the fire.

A bright fire was burning; not one of those depressing affairs which depend upon logs for an uneasy flame and a trickle of smoke but a business-like fire of logs and coal combined; a fire built to warm and cheer.

On a rug in front of the fire a Corgi dog lay, looking like a cylindrical woolly bear, and pricked his ears when I came in.

I liked the look of the tray of drinks on a side-table, and wondered whether Bartels had supplied them, and paid for them, at trade prices. She gave me a whisky and soda, and helped herself to a gin-and-Italian. I drank the whisky without a qualm.

I didn't care if Bartels had paid for them or not. I had come to steal his woman, and I was quite prepared to drink his drink while I did so. If you are going to set fire to a man's house, there's no sense in feeling awkward because your cigarette end has singed his mantelpiece.

I had laid my plans carefully, and I felt confident. I was better looking than Bartels – not good-looking, but better looking than Bartels. For one thing I didn't wear spectacles, and I was better built physically. I had a quicker wit, more experience of the world; and I had a far wider experience of women. Bartels had almost no experience of women.

I was good with women. I knew that most men try to impress women by talking about themselves. They try to show themselves in a clever light, shoot a line, preen their feathers. Women like this for a short while. Then it bores them.

A woman is seriously attracted to the man who talks, not about himself, but about women in general and about her in particular. This never bores her. Nor does it ever bore me to talk about an attractive woman, on the rare occasions when I am with one.

So that's the way I played it, during the first part of that first evening with Lorna Dickson.

Within a few minutes, by asking questions about silver-framed photographs on the mantelpiece and occasional tables, I had her talking about her family and her own affairs.

Her father, Major Clive Burton, M.C., had been killed during the First World War. Her mother, who had a flair for dressmaking, and a circle of friends and acquaintances in the Woking area, had set herself up in business and had built up a reasonable clientele. It was not a flourishing business, not a big money-maker, but it brought in a steady income. And there was a little money from her father's estate.

There was one other child, Leslie Burton, who was a chartered accountant.

Lorna had helped her mother in the business until she was twenty-three. Then she had married Ronald Dickson, a rubber-planter on leave from Malaya, and in 1938 had sailed with him to Singapore.

Two years later, under protest, but because he wished it, she had sailed for home alone. He had stayed, in the face of the gathering storm, and had been engulfed.

She never saw him again.

She never heard from him again, or, for a long time, received any firm news about him. Only once, through roundabout means, through a friend who had a friend who had fought with Ronnie Dickson, she heard a story that he had last been seen drifting down a river on a raft; wounded, but in good heart. Later, a story trickled through that he had been drowned.

'So I only had him for two years,' she said, standing by the mantelpiece looking down into the fire. 'Not long, but by heavens it was worth it. I don't regret a moment of my life.'

'You're lucky,' I said.

She looked at me and smiled. 'Why? Do you?'

'Lots. Did you never think of marrying again? I mean, until recently.'

She side-stepped the reference to Bartels. She said:

'I had no wish to. I joined the W A A F s, and spent most of the war on a crag in Scotland. Hoping, of course. Watching the post every day for a Red Cross letter, or something. Suspense like that is bad. But it gives you a chance to reconcile your mind.'

'I suppose so.'

'I used to cry a good deal at night, at first, especially after I heard the rumours that he had been drowned. But that stopped, too, after a while; and then there was only a sort of dull pain left.'

'And now that's gone, too?'

She shook her head. 'No, it hasn't. I don't think it ever will, really. There was no disillusionment. The star-dust was still sprinkled over our marriage when he died.'

'He's all right now,' I said, after a little while. 'He wouldn't want you to go on feeling that pain.'

'Oh, I know that. But you can't just command yourself not to feel something. When the rumours were confirmed at the end of the war, I thought: well, this is the end. I've had my life, or all of it that matters. Have another whisky?'

'Thank you, I will.'

She went across to the table and filled our glasses.

'After the war, I came back here, and lived with Mother and Leslie. Then Leslie married and moved to London, and three years ago Mother died. So here I am. That's my life to date.'

She smiled at me. I smiled back. I said:

'You know, when you come to the end of your life, I have a feeling you'll find it has been divided into four periods: the period of youth, the period of happiness, the period of trial, and the period of renewed happiness. That's what you'll find. I'm sure of it.'

I wasn't being crafty now. It hurt me to think of her pain and sadness. I would have done anything to comfort her: anything, that is, except let Bartels have her.

He never had a chance after I had made up my mind to have her. Not a cat in hell's chance.

'You're going through the trial period now, Lorna. But hang on. It's only a question of hanging on. Do believe me.'

'I hope so.'

She smiled at me again. Again I smiled back, and this time I held her eyes with my own for about as long as it takes a man to draw a quick, deep breath. And that in fact is what I was doing at the sight of the beauty of Lorna's eyes.

Then I looked away, into the fire, because a voice, the

crudely tongued voice which often prompts me, was whispering in my brain: softee, softee, catchee bloody monkey – don't flirt, or you'll frighten her off; she'll think you're a wolf, which you often are, but never mind: softee, softee, catchee bloody monkey. . . .

I'm cunning with women, I've got a kind of knack of seeming gentle, and sympathetic, and understanding, and all that sort of thing. And to some degree I think I must be, because you can't act those qualities successfully for long: not well enough to deceive women, who are pretty cunning themselves, if it comes to that.

This sounds conceited, but it can't be helped. It is the truth as I see it, and I've got to mention it or otherwise, in view of what happened, Lorna will appear to have been a pretty poor type. Fickle. A bit of a bitch. Which she wasn't. Like Bartels, she never had a chance, once I got going on her.

There is another side to me, too. I'm interested in everybody, and I've made it my business to learn how to play on them, to draw emotions and reactions from them as the bow draws the notes from a fiddle. Against the softer side of my nature, there is a calculating, ruthless, cool streak.

So now I looked away, and did not flirt. Then suddenly, I said, as though it were something which had just occurred to me:

'What about coming out for a bite of dinner? What about driving over to the Crown, at Chiddingfold? Come on, it'll make a change for you.'

I waited for her answer, feeling tense despite my previous confidence.

'Well, I think I'd like to,' said Lorna.

When she said that, I knew she was in the bag.

*

But I took it easy that night.

To begin with, I was overjoyed to be dining alone with her, and it was not until we had finished dinner and were having coffee and liqueurs, seated in the bar-lounge in one of the deep settees near the fire, that we touched upon the subject of Bartels.

Indeed, it was Lorna who broached the subject, with a typically direct question:

'What is wrong with Barty's marriage?' she asked suddenly, and leant forward to refill the coffee-cups.

'Most men would say there is nothing wrong with it,' I answered. 'But there is, of course.'

'Whose fault is it?'

I hesitated. 'Nobody's,' I said at length. 'Nobody's, really.'

I had assumed that Lorna would automatically believe that Beatrice was in the wrong, but I misjudged that eminently well-balanced and fair-minded character. Perhaps I had also misjudged Bartels, for I thought he would have played the role of the husband who was not understood by his wife. Her next words showed me that this was not so.

'That's what Barty says,' she agreed. 'He says nobody is to blame, really.' She hesitated and added: 'The trouble with Barty is that he is a man who depends upon emotions for his happiness, and he is married to a woman who depends upon material conditions – possessions. Both of them are good people, fundamentally.'

'That's the tragedy.'

'Barty's trouble is that he has never had anyone in love with him.'

'Until now,' I said, and looked at her. 'You know he is very much in love with you, of course, and I assume that you are in love with him. Right?'

It is curious that both of the women in Bartels' life were

incapable of telling lies. Lorna looked at me now and said:

'I don't know.'

'Well, for God's sake! I thought you were both deeply in love and couldn't do without each other.'

She stared past me into the fire. She said nothing, I listened to the low murmur of conversation from other people in the lounge and said nothing. And waited.

'The trouble is,' she said at last, 'I still have my memories of Ronnie. I can't seem to shake them off. But I am so lonely, you know. People think a woman needs to be loved and that is true, but it is not the whole truth. She also needs somebody to love.'

'Hence Poodles and Pekes.'

'Hence Poodles and Pekes. Barty loves me and needs me. I can't quite see why, but I accept the fact. In a way, I suppose I am terribly grateful to him for loving me.'

'He thinks you're in love with him,' I said. And when she said nothing, I said again, more slowly and distinctly:

'He thinks you're in *love* with him.'

She still said nothing, and I purposely did not look at her because I did not wish either to press her or to embarrass her. I was in love with her, and my heart went out to her as she tried to fathom her own feelings. I felt like saying: Don't bother to explain, darling, I know it all.

Instead, the calculating side of my mind was at work: the side that plotted carefully, planned to get what it wanted and nearly always succeeded. So I said, with deceptive gentleness:

'Gratitude is perhaps an insecure foundation on which to build a life with Barty. He wants more.'

'And he would have more,' she retorted quickly, almost sharply. I retreated at once.

'I'm sure he would.'

'I do love the man. You don't seem to realize that. I

107

want to look after him, as he wants to look after me. I want to pour out on him love and tenderness and affection. I think he is hurt and disillusioned, and I want to heal him.'

A stab of jealousy and pain went through me.

'Very laudable. I'm sure you can do it.'

'Well, then?' she looked at me. I smiled and signalled to the waiter.

'Well, then – have another brandy?' I smiled at her, and offered her my cigarette-case. She refused both the brandy and the cigarette. I ordered another drink for myself, put the cigarette-case away and began to fill my pipe.

'Well?' she said again.

'Well, what?'

'Do you think I am wrong to wish to marry him?'

'I am not the judge of your conscience, and when I say that, I am not thinking of his wife. I am thinking of him. Perhaps of you, too.'

'I can make him happy. Happier than he has been. He is such a lovable chap,' she said, almost sadly, 'I do so want to make him happy.'

I felt a little tug at my heart: I, too, was fond of old Barty. For some reason, I thought of him as I had first known him at school; being rolled in the mat, and pushed under the vaulting horse; and watching, pale-faced, from the school window until he could safely come out and run home. But I couldn't afford to indulge in that line of thought for long.

'Look at me,' I said quietly, and when she had turned her head to face me, I said: 'Are you in love with Barty?'

'I love him dearly.'

I shook my head. 'Are you in love with him?'

When she hesitated, I dropped my little seed of doubt into the rich kindly soil of her heart, and left it to take root and bear fruit, if so it would.

'Actually, although she is not in love with him,' I said,

quite casually, as though it were of no importance, 'although she is certainly not *in love* with him, Beatrice loves him, too, in her own way. She'll take it hardly, I fear. I wouldn't care to do what Bartels is going to do.'

*

All the evening I was playing the decent fellow with Lorna; the sympathetic friend, the disinterested adviser; talking of all sorts of things as I drove her home along the frosty roads, back to the house in the lane where she lived; making her laugh now and again; interesting her with stories about the seamy side of big hotels; talking of travels abroad, and, at the end, saying how much I had enjoyed the evening.

I did not even accept her invitation to go into the house for a final drink.

I said good-bye to her on the porch, shaking hands almost primly, even though I longed to take her in my arms and crush her to me, and light the light of passion in her eyes, and feel the softness of her lips on mine, and the warm suppleness of her body.

I was taking no risks.

I wanted her so badly for my own that every nerve and brain-cell was alert in my head, and the voice was crying, softee, softee, catchee monkey, and I knew I must be patient or lose her.

Chapter 11

THEY say that jealousy is caused by fear, or a lack of self-confidence, or a feeling of insecurity; but I am under the impression that I felt supremely confident in so far as Lorna was concerned. Nevertheless, I felt the pangs of jealousy most acutely.

In the six days that followed, I visited Lorna on two other occasions, and each time I acted with circumspection, well knowing that to attempt to hasten matters would result in showing me to be the false friend that, in fact, I was. But, on each occasion, I contrived to let fall some further hint, some little indication that Beatrice, in her own way, loved Bartels; that for Lorna to encourage a divorce without being romantically in love with Bartels would merely cause him, in the end, to feel the same sense of frustration as he felt at the moment.

In this, I think that I was correct, though I did not act out of a sense of what was right, but simply because I desired the woman for myself. I would have done the same even had I thought I was wrong.

The jealousy which I felt naturally attacked me most fiercely on those evenings when I knew, by one means or another, that Bartels was with her.

It wasn't any use telling myself that I was a better man than Bartels, and that in the end I would win. I knew it. But it did not prevent pictures forming in my mind. Pictures of Bartels with his arm round Lorna, on the settee in her comfortable drawing-room; of Bartels spending long hours with Lorna's head upon his shoulder, his hand on hers, while the fat roly-poly Corgi dozed in front of the fire.

Worst, of course, was the almost unbearable thought of

Bartels kissing her, and her lips responding, of Bartels taking her in his arms and telling her how much he loved her.

It came to the point that, when I met Bartels, the sight of his wide mouth, which had formerly only amused me, now filled me with disgust. A dull, painful anger burned in my stomach at the thought that those colourless, thin lips should ever be allowed to press upon Lorna's mouth.

On such evenings, when I knew they were together, I would find myself compelled to go out, to a theatre, or a cinema; anywhere, rather than remain at home and imagine what was going on at Thatchley. Sometimes, out of a morbid sense of twisted humour, I would call on Beatrice.

Beatrice suspected nothing.

She was accustomed to him going away for two or three nights a week on a provincial tour selling his wines. She trusted him completely, and she was convinced that, whatever her emotional failings, he needed her and his well-being depended upon her; that without her, without her organizing ability, her strength of mind, he would be miserable and lost. There was no doubt in her mind on that score whatever. She made this clear to me many times in casual little remarks.

'I don't know where he'd be if he hadn't me to organize him a bit,' she would say, affectionately. Then she would sigh a little and smile. Right up to the end, to the time when he went to Manchester and bought the altrapeine with which to poison her, and even later, Beatrice Bartels thought that her husband needed her.

So much for women's intuition. I never believed much in it. I believe even less now.

On Friday afternoon, 23 February, I decided to drive down to Bartels' cottage. I knew that Bartels would be with Lorna all that afternoon and early evening, and the thought of it, as usual, filled me with a restless resentment.

I lunched at my club, but my mood was such that the food was repulsive to me, and I left a great deal of it untouched. After lunch I strolled into the smoking-room, and ordered coffee and a brandy. I tried to read some papers and periodicals, but found nothing in them to interest me.

Such people as I talked to bored me, and I have no doubt that I bored them, too.

I felt so restless that I got up and went into the billiards room, and played a game with the marker. I played abominably. My imagination was at work, my mind was elsewhere. I was thinking that at any moment Bartels would be arriving. I could see him drawing up at the front door in his old twelve-horse-power car, and Lorna Dickson greeting him on the threshold.

I could see them going into the drawing-room together, and sitting together. I could see Bartels fondling her, and the sight of it so disturbed me that in the middle of the game I suddenly walked to the end of the room and returned my cue to the stand.

The marker looked at me curiously. I made some excuse about an appointment, but it was clear that he thought I was suffering from pique at my lack of skill – not that it mattered a damn to me what he was thinking.

The theatre and cinema guide showed nothing which appealed to me. So on the spur of the moment, I decided to drive down to Bartels' week-end cottage, near Balcombe. I would take advantage of the open invitation which was extended to me, and spend the night with them. Beatrice, I knew, would be there, and possibly I would take her to a local hotel, in the early evening, where we could usually find one or two people we knew.

At the back of my mind was the thought that I would know exactly when he had returned from visiting Lorna:

directly I was certain he was no longer with her, my peace of mind would return.

I drove back to my flat, packed a few things in a suitcase, and set off. I wish a thousand times, now, that I had not gone.

But I could not have foreseen what I would find there, or the quandary in which I would be placed.

You reached the cottage by one of two ways. You could either follow the road round, and turn in at the front gate and arrive at the front door, or you could turn off down a narrower road, leave the car, pass through a small gate at the bottom of the garden, and walk up through the vegetable gardens, via the tree-fringed lawn, and enter the house by the french windows, in summer, or else by way of the kitchen door. This was a shorter route.

The cottage lay in a hollow, and although you had to slow up a little to take the turning into the narrower road, you could, with a certain amount of luck and dash, coast down the last three or four hundred yards with the engine switched off. If you slowed up in the slightest degree before reaching the corner, perhaps to pass a cyclist, you lost just enough momentum to necessitate switching the engine on again.

But nothing got in my way that day, and I coasted down to the back gate, feeling the usual childish pleasure which one experiences after minor triumphs of this kind.

It was a beautiful evening, cold but cloudless, and the day was just fading when I arrived. The sun had set, but there was a red blaze still in the sky beyond the wood by the side of the cottage.

I sat for a moment relaxing, for I had driven fast, and the speed and the control of the car had done me good, and for a while I had even forgotten Bartels and Lorna. I sucked in the clean, cold air, and wondered why the devil I lived in London.

A horse neighed in the distance, and some rooks were still cawing their belated way home. I could see the warm glow of a fire shining through the windows of the drawing-room, and guessed that Beatrice, good housewife and efficient as ever, would have tea ready for anybody who might call in. Ready, even, for Barty, I thought bitterly.

It was all wonderfully peaceful and, with the vision it conjured up of muffins and toast, essentially English. The scene was not one in which to anticipate a shock of any kind, but the shock was awaiting me. Not a shock evoked by violence, by murder, or physical wounding, but a pretty big shock all the same.

I climbed out of the car, and as I did so a little wind sprang up and shook the trees at the bottom of the garden. The door by the driving-seat had sunk a trifle on its hinges, so that instead of slamming it I had to lift it slightly and push it shut.

I wish now that I had had that hinge repaired when I had first intended, days before, but I had postponed doing so. It might have saved me a good deal of heartache, and, I suppose – remorse.

I passed through the vegetable garden, walking along the side, on the grass path, and so came to the little lawn, with the trellis-work and ramblers which partly screened off the vegetable garden.

There were a few apple and pear trees on each side of the lawn, and I followed the grass path through them, and came to a gravel path, which ran round the back of the house. It was an old path, still damp from the morning's rain, and very mossy in places.

I thought of going round to the kitchen door, but instead crossed the path and went up to the french windows, thinking that Beatrice could let me in.

The blazing fire lit up the room, but otherwise there was

no lighting. I could see the deep arm-chairs near the fire, and the writing-table in the window with its silver ink-pots, and two little carved ivory elephants; and the glass-fronted bookcase against one wall, and the corner cupboard where they kept the drinks.

I could also see, at an angle to the window, the big settee, and Beatrice upon it, her arms round the neck of a man whose lips were pressed upon hers. He was bending over her, and because the top of his head was towards me, and the light was dim, I did not recognize John O'Brien until, after some seconds, and for some reason unknown, he looked up and saw me.

I heard him murmur something to Beatrice, and saw him stand up and automatically straighten his tie and smooth his dark hair with his hands. I saw Beatrice sit bolt upright, suddenly and quickly, and she, too, put her hands to her hair.

It was difficult to know what to do. I had a quick tempting thought that it might be better to walk away, back to the car, as though I had seen nothing; and greet them some other day as though the incident had never happened.

I might have done so, except that even while I hesitated the first dim realization of what this involved for me was beginning to emerge.

I decided to compromise, to walk round to the kitchen door, slowly, giving them time to recover, and then allow John or Beatrice to make the running. If they said nothing, I would be content to say nothing, at any rate for the time being.

I moved away from the window, but I had not gone more than two or three paces when the french window was opened, and John's voice called :

'Hey, Pete!'

I looked round, and tried to put a surprised tone into my voice.

'Why, hullo, John! I was just descending upon Beatrice and Barty for a breath of fresh air.'

'The Assyrian came down like a wolf on the fold,' said John, with a bitter little laugh. 'Well, come in this way.'

'Thanks,' I said and retraced my steps, and entered the drawing-room by the french window which he was holding open for me.

Beatrice was standing by the fire.

'Hullo, Beatrice,' I said. 'Got a bed for a poor London sparrow with soot in his lungs?'

'Of course I have, Pete. You know that, or you wouldn't be here.'

In the incredibly quick way in which women can do these things, she had managed to straighten her hair and clothes, and even plump up the cushions on the settee, all within the few seconds which had elapsed since I had turned away from the french windows.

She stood with her hands behind her back, her fine hazel eyes meeting mine without flinching. She was smiling, in friendly and hospitable fashion. Only her chin was a little higher than usual. There followed a short conversation which, in the circumstances, was the most futile I have ever taken part in. We were all trying so desperately hard to appear normal. The only real normal living creature in the room was the dog, Brutus. Sleepy with age, he lay with his big, square, white-and-brown bulk stretched out before the fire.

'God, what a lovely evening,' I said.

'Isn't it, absolutely heavenly?' said Beatrice.

'Should be fine tomorrow, too, judging by the sunset,' said John.

'I don't know why I live in London,' I said.

'Nor me,' said John. 'Why not make the break, like I did?'

'Maybe I will, one day.'

'Have you had tea?' asked Beatrice.

'Not yet.'

'I'll put the kettle on.'

'Don't make it specially for me.'

'We haven't had any yet, either.'

'I could do with a cup,' said John, and I thought: that doesn't surprise me, either, brother.

'Or even two,' said John facetiously. Or even, I thought, a bloody great whisky and soda, but that's just what you can't have, because it's too early.

'And some toast,' John plunged on bravely. 'Lashings of toast. Eh, Beatrice?'

Maybe it was a case of telepathy, because he paused for a moment, and then said: 'Or would you prefer a whisky and soda, to warm you up after your drive? I expect Beatrice could provide it.'

I suppose he would have made some pretext to join me in one, to judge by the hopeful way he was looking at me.

'I think I'd just as soon have a cup of tea, thanks,' I said.

There was a pause. Beatrice moved to the door.

'I'll take my bag up to my room,' I said at last.

I went upstairs. Beatrice went into the kitchen to put the kettle on. After a few moments, I heard John join her, and they talked in low tones. I began to unpack, very slowly, for I wanted to give them time to sort things out. After about a quarter of an hour I went down to the drawing-room, and found tea laid out on a gate-legged table before the fire.

Beatrice and John were sitting side by side on the settee, eating crumpets. I sat down in one of the deep arm-chairs, and helped myself to a crumpet from the dish which John passed to me. Beatrice poured me out a cup of tea.

Nobody spoke for about two minutes, and I thought: they're going to have the matter out with me. If they weren't, they would have started to talk trivialities. They are going to get down to business. I waited patiently for one or other of them to make a move.

John spoke first. He wiped some butter from his lips with his pocket handkerchief, and drained his tea-cup, and replaced it on the table, and turned his rather heavy red face towards me and said:

'Well, now you know, don't you?'

'Know what?'

'Now you know how things stand between Beatrice and me.'

I hesitated. 'Yes,' I said, 'yes, I do.'

He nodded. Beatrice was looking down at her finger-nails, hands in her lap.

'At least,' I added, 'I know how things appear to stand. But appearances can be deceptive. I saw you kissing her, if that's what you mean.'

'That is exactly what I mean.'

'Yes, well, it's no business of mine,' I went on. 'I'm not married to Beatrice. It's no concern of mine to cause trouble. Beatrice is not the first girl to have a bit of a flirtation in her husband's absence.'

Neither of them said anything.

'As far as I'm concerned,' I finished. 'I've seen nothing. The fire-light can play strange tricks. It's not for me to pass on stories which could be based on a figment of the imagination.'

In my opinion it was a pretty fair offer. I had not yet become fully involved personally in the implications of what I had seen.

Beatrice wouldn't have it that way. Beatrice, the courageous, the clear thinker, the woman who faced every issue fairly and squarely, declined the easy escape.

'It is not a flirtation,' she said, flatly. 'I'm in love with John. And he says he's in love with me. That is the position.'

The lamp-light fell on her red hair, and in the same light her skin looked creamy white and rose. She looked beautiful and very seductive. There was no trace of shame in her demeanour. There was no tremor in her voice. Yet to call her shameless would be unfair; she was more a fearless woman who recognized that a certain situation had arisen and was prepared to cope with the consequences.

'That's the position,' she said again, when I remained quiet.

'I suppose you're quite sure?' I asked.

'Quite sure,' replied John firmly, and loudly.

'Absolutely,' said Beatrice.

'Divorce?' I said, looking directly at Beatrice. I saw John place his hand over hers on the settee, and surmised that the subject had been pretty thoroughly discussed.

She shook her head. 'No, no divorce.'

'Not – ever?' I said.

'No, not ever. I made a bargain with Barty, and I'll keep it. If I thought he didn't need me so much, I think – well, I think I would. But I'm all he's got to hang on to, you know. His job is a bit of a failure.'

She reached forward to toss a log on to the fire. Then:

'I'm still very fond of him, you know. And I can't stand the thought of what he might do if I left him.'

'Do you mean he might commit suicide?'

'Not so much that.'

'What, then?'

Beatrice made a vague little gesture with her hand. 'Oh, I don't know. Drink, perhaps. And his clothes would all go to pot. And he might get the sack. Or get caught on the rebound by some untidy little slut who would drag him down.'

'What do you think, John?' I looked at him.

I had always liked old John, with his Irish lightheartedness, even though I had thought he was rather self-indulgent

119

in matters of food and wine. I thought he might oppose her.

'Beatrice knows him best,' said John softly. 'She honestly thinks that Barty would go to pieces without her. She may be right. The poor chap hasn't had much fun out of life.'

I felt my heart beginning to beat faster. In a few words I could set their consciences at rest, make them two of the happiest people in England, and settle Barty's problem for him, too.

'I'm so terribly sorry for him,' said Beatrice suddenly. 'I remember not long ago he returned late one night, very cold and tired. I had written him a little note to cheer him up, and left it with a mince-pie. I heard him read the note as I lay in bed, half asleep. Then he got into his bed, and I put out my hand to him, and in the end he went to sleep. He was so cold and tired, you know. I was glad he didn't have to come back to an empty flat. That's what would happen if I went away with John.'

'He works too hard,' said John, and got up to put another log on the fire. 'And it doesn't get him anywhere. That's the trouble. He'll never make a really good salesman.'

'Too modest,' said Beatrice. 'Too modest and gentle. I think I could do it, if he was a real success, if he was making lots of money.'

'As it is, you can't,' said John. 'That's ironic, really. He's a failure at his job, and because he is a failure he's a success with the one person in the world who matters. Queer, isn't it?'

Beatrice caught the bitterness in his voice.

She reached out and gripped his hand and held it tight, and looked up at him.

I thought: Bartels was right. There is indeed one man in the world with whom she can be in love, and now she has found him.

But by now, ruthless as ever in the pursuit of that which I desired, I had made up my mind what to do. Just as I had planted and watered a seed of doubt in Lorna's mind, so now I crushed all generous thoughts about revealing the true position to Beatrice and John O'Brien. For if Philip Bartels obtained his freedom from Beatrice, I should lose Lorna.

I had no intention of losing Lorna.

Doubtless Bartels, that over-kind man, would have acted differently. But Bartels was a failure in life. I was not. So I did not hesitate for long.

I spoke quietly and a little sadly, in the tone of voice of one who has deliberated deeply, and has come to the conclusion that however unpleasant his decision it must nevertheless be announced: the old family friend doing his stuff: the trusted adviser, impartial and benevolent, throwing his opinion into the scales. What hypocrisy it was!

'Would you like my views?' I asked mildly. And before they could reply I continued: 'I think – I'm afraid Beatrice is right.'

She turned quickly and looked at me, and then looked away. It was only a glance, yet I thought I caught a flash of pain behind her eyes: as though she had hoped, in spite of all she had said, that I would counter her arguments with some of my own.

I thought I saw, too, a tinge of despair. As if all hope were now indeed lost. I regretted it, but it did not deter me.

'I think he would be pretty lost without Beatrice,' I said. 'I think he would certainly try to kill the pain in some fashion, quite possibly with drink. And I think that he might well end up by losing his job. He's hardly indispensable in the firm, is he?'

Beatrice said: 'Thank you for being frank.'

John said nothing for a moment. Then he said:

'Don't you think he might marry again? Some nice woman or other? Don't you think he might?'

I heard the note of urgency in his voice, and recognized

it as a kind of last desperate appeal. One half of my mind was sorry for the poor chap. The other half, the part that looked after my own interests, was completely unmoved.

'No, I don't,' I said flatly. And to ram the point well home I added: 'I don't think he would ever fall in love again. And don't forget – I've known him since childhood.'

I got up and walked over to the window and stood looking out into the darkness. The wind had risen, and the trees were tossing against the night sky. I thought that in three hours, perhaps less, Bartels would be no longer with Lorna. Kissing her and fondling her. Pawing her. Mouthing phrases like a lovesick youth. Kissing her . . . kissing her . . . kissing her again. The wave of jealousy mounted higher and higher inside me.

I clenched my fists in my trouser pockets, and swung round again to Beatrice and John.

'I don't think there is the slightest chance that he would marry again,' I said loudly and harshly. They thought, no doubt, that I sounded stern because I was concerned about Bartels' well-being. Poor simpletons!

*

He came back about 9.30 that evening: Philip Bartels, my friend. Beatrice was very nice to him, and he was very nice to her.

He was glad to see me, too. He said so.

I didn't know that in an inside pocket of his overcoat was a bottle marked Aspirins, that it had been there for some days, or that the contents bore not the slightest resemblance to aspirins.

Chapter 12

I SHALL always remember that Saturday, because as it turned out it was the last day which Philip and Beatrice Bartels and I spent together.

I did not know that, of course, and there was nothing to indicate it. It began as one of those days which make you think that winter is past, and that spring is not very far ahead; the sun shone out of a brittle blue sky, dazzlingly bright, and the sprinkling of frost on the lawn sparkled and danced in the pale, intense light.

I always sleep with the windows partly open, but when I got up that morning, I opened them wider still, and looked out, and breathed in deeply and felt glad to be alive.

The air was cold, and as I was not even wearing a dressing-gown, it penetrated quickly to my skin, and raced over my face and neck and chest, yet left behind no feeling of chill, but rather a tingling, invigorating feeling as though I had been massaged.

It was quite late, past nine o'clock, for the Bartels took things very easily at week-ends, as is right and proper, and we usually wandered down for breakfast at about a quarter to ten.

A robin fluttered down on to the lawn, hopped a few paces and stood listening. Somebody, presumably Beatrice, was moving about in the kitchen handling crockery.

The air was very still; so still that when the dog Brutus wandered out of the french windows below me, I picked up the sound as his heavy body disturbed the pebbles on the path.

The dog Brutus moved slowly on to the lawn, took a few paces and stopped, and stretched, his forelegs thrust out before him, tensing his hind legs in turn. The robin took no notice, as though aware that so old and heavy a body was incapable of sudden and dangerous attack.

The dog lowered his head to the ground, and sniffed, and then raised his half-blind eyes to the sun; his head moved slowly from side to side, as though he were trying to discern the source of the rays which were warming his body. He took a few more steps, and stood uncertainly looking across the lawn to where the vegetable garden lay.

'Brutus!' I called. 'Hello, Brutus, boy!'

The dog took no notice, so I called louder: 'Brutus! Hello, boy!'

The dog turned his heavy head and peered in the direction from which my voice had come. His stump of a tail moved gently from side to side, then he turned his head away and continued to gaze down the garden.

I thought: he is so old now that he does not much care whether human company is around or not; he is a half-numbed entity, for whom the hours and the days bring either warmth and comfort, or cold and discomfort; either food and satisfaction or vague stirrings of hunger and restlessness.

Men come to it, like dogs: but men have their memories, to amuse and comfort them, or to torture and plague them. Memory is a mixed blessing. Time soothes most of the wounds of the past, but the ugliest remain unhealed; perhaps they are even exacerbated by the play of the imagination. Dogs don't suffer like that. Dogs die easy deaths, devoid of hopes or fears. It's a consolation for having to eat the half-cold remains from people's plates, I thought.

I closed the window, and bathed and dressed, and went down to breakfast. Beatrice and Barty were already at table, reading the newspapers. There were boiled eggs for breakfast, two each, for Beatrice, efficient as ever, had good local contacts.

We did not talk much. I think that each of them was conscious that I shared his or her secret, that bright February morning. As for me, I was merely concerned that neither should discern the true feelings of the other.

Of the two, as I thought even then, Beatrice was the finer character; she had made her bargain, married without being in love; but having made it she was going to keep it, even though it nearly broke her heart to do so.

Not so Philip Bartels. Unless I could prevent it, he was going to break what he considered to have been a bad bargain, and marry Lorna.

Such being the case, I had to take swift action in two directions. I had to consolidate the position in regard to Beatrice and John O'Brien, and I had to see Lorna Dickson and strengthen the idea that it would be wrong of her to take Bartels from Beatrice.

Yet all my plans were put in peril in a most unexpected way that same morning.

To begin with everything went according to plan. After breakfast, Bartels went out into the garden to fix a piece of trellis-work that had come loose in the night, and I offered to help Beatrice with the washing-up.

Beatrice washed the things. I dried them. At first we did not speak; each knew the subject which lay uppermost in the other's mind; each was reluctant to broach the subject, or perhaps Beatrice, like myself, did not know how to start.

At length, as I was drying the last few knives, I said abruptly:

'I have thought some more about you and John.'

'What have you thought?'

She turned her head and looked at me anxiously. I did not know whether she was hopeful that I might have changed my mind, in order that she could have some moral backing for reconsidering the problem herself, or whether, having now reconciled herself, she was fearful lest I put up arguments which would cause her to weaken.

'I think that you and John are well suited to each other, but I am not at all certain that one can build happiness upon the unhappiness of somebody else.'

'I suppose not,' she said. 'I suppose you're right.'

'Some people could, but not you, Beatrice dear. Not a person with your burden of conscience.'

'No.'

She wiped her right hand on her apron, and then pushed some hair back from her forehead. The blood had mounted to her head, and her lower lip was trembling. She raised her hand again, and brushed it across her eyes.

'I wish I could advise you otherwise. I would willingly sacrifice Barty, if I thought that you and John would be happy.'

She stood at the sink, saying nothing, cleaning a small glass marmalade dish with a small mop, pushing the mop round and round.

'John might be happy,' I went on, 'but not you, Beatrice dear. Your thoughts would go out to Barty, all the time, souring everything. Perhaps even embittering your relationship with John.'

The winter sunlight shone through the little window, touching her beautiful red hair. Once, she looked quickly at me and tried to smile, and I saw the tears in her eyes. She nodded her head, with that quick little trembling smile, and bent over the sink again. And all the time, forgetful of what she was doing, she continued to push the little mop round the marmalade dish.

For a moment, despite my resolution, I felt sick at heart, not merely at her heartbreak, but at my own treachery.

I saw her standing, almost symbolically, at the sink, a woman who had been faced with the greatest temptation which a married woman can encounter. But because her conception of duty, of what is fair and decent, was so strong, she had won her struggle.

I suddenly flung the dish-cloth over the back of a chair, and murmured an apology and went out of the kitchen.

I was nauseated by my own actions. 'Beatrice dear,' I had called her. 'I wish I could advise you otherwise,' I had said. And with it all, I had spoken in a low, regretful tone, as though the one thing I longed for was to be able to tell her something different. I went into the drawing-room, and paced up and down in front of the fireplace.

I couldn't go on with it.

I was not as tough as I thought I was. This was the invisible 'X', the unseen factor which was going to upset my plans.

I had the power to make three people happier than they had ever been before, and one person reasonably happy. As is so often the case with ruthless people like myself, I was swept by a wave of the most revolting sentimentality.

I conjured up mental pictures of Bartels, with his gentle smile, and quiet good nature, and diffident manner; Bartels, the unsuccessful wine salesman, traipsing round the countryside, longing for Lorna, whom he believed to be in love with him, and who would certainly never let him see that she was not.

I thought of Beatrice, whose heart called out for the strong masculinity of John O'Brien; Beatrice who was fundamentally so good that she was prepared to sacrifice her own happiness rather than harm, as she thought, a devoted and dependent husband.

Even the forceful and sturdy John O'Brien came in for his share of my pity: John, fundamentally decent, too, who was prepared to stand by Beatrice's decision, whatever the cost to himself. John, the good-humoured, the generous, the kind.

The wave of sentimentality receded.

In its place I felt quite cool. I lit a cigarette, and threw the match in the fireplace, and stood smoking and looking out of the window. Bartels had apparently finished his work on the trellis, and must have gone down to the vegetable garden, for he was no longer in sight.

I had never imagined that I would be prepared to sacrifice my own ambitions for anybody else, not even for Beatrice and Bartels.

But that is what I now proposed to do.

I walked to the door and into the passage and along to the kitchen. My heart was beating a little faster than usual, but I was determined. Beatrice had finished the drying-up, and was going over the floor with a mop. The back door was open. The dog Brutus lay dozing on the mat.

I stood by the kitchen door in silence for a few seconds, watching her.

'Beatrice,' I said, at last, and now I had come to it the word had to be forced through my lips. She looked up, but said nothing.

'Beatrice,' I said again. She stopped mopping the floor and looked round at me. A wisp of hair had fallen over one eye. She looked listless and tired.

'Yes?'

Curiously enough, at that moment I felt a surge of happiness within me. Even at this late date, I can still recall a faint flavour of it. It was the unalloyed, pure joy which only a giver can know.

For a second I hesitated, looking upon Beatrice's unhappy face and anticipating the wild happiness I was going to bring to her. Yet I wasn't feeling smug, or virtuous: just happy. It was most odd.

But the dog Brutus raised his head.

I heard the sound of a footstep, then a noise as Bartels kicked some mud off his shoes on the scraper. Then he came into the kitchen. And I thought of him, with Lorna, his wide, colourless lips pressed on hers; his deep musical voice, in such contrast to his appearance, murmuring endearments. I imagined him married to her and all that that implied. It was too much for me.

'Beatrice,' I said loudly, 'let's go along to the local for a drink at twelve. What about it?'

If Bartels had stayed outside two minutes more, so much might have been changed.

*

We did not go to the local. Beatrice said she had to stay and watch the joint. It was my joint. I always brought a joint for the week-ends. There is no point in being in the hotel business if one cannot scrounge a reasonably sized joint for oneself now and again.

But Bartels asked me to come for a stroll across the fields with Brutus. I went with him willingly enough, for the wave of jealousy was still around me, and the foolish, generous weakness had been replaced by the old well-known feeling of determination to fight for what I wanted by fair means and, if necessary, by foul ones – in that order.

I thought I did quite well during that walk, for I made him promise that he would not leave Beatrice until Easter, pointing out to him that at that time she would be spending a fortnight with her parents in Falmouth, and that the blow would be softened if she were with her family.

He promised readily enough.

In view of what he had in mind, I am not surprised.

I recall now, incidentally, how kind he was to the dog Brutus during that walk. Indeed, he had been unusually kind to the dog at breakfast, feeding him with tit-bits from the table, a thing he never normally allowed, and caressing him.

So now, upon that beautiful February morning, Bartels led the dog along hedgerows where a scent of rabbits could perhaps be detected, encouraging him with soft words, and sometimes calling him for a pat. And once we went through a small copse, because sometimes a cock pheasant lurked in the undergrowth.

The dog Brutus seemed for a space to regain some of his youthful vigour, and though he could not move fast, he showed all his former enthusiasm, and snuffled in the hedges and among the briars, tail wagging; and once, when he put a rabbit up, he lumbered after it excitedly, until shortness of breath made him abandon the chase after a few yards.

Bartels was quieter than usual, and I noticed in the bright sunlight certain lines upon his face, and a suggestion of a shadow under the eyes, which I had not seen before.

He talked to me of his future plans for Lorna and himself; how Lorna, at least for a while, would have to continue with her dressmaking.

'But she says she doesn't mind,' he said.

'She is not the sort of woman who would,' I answered. And I thought that if I had my way, and I was sure I would, Lorna would never make another dress as long as she lived, except for her own pleasure.

'But I hope it won't be for long,' said Bartels.

'You do?'

'She is the kind of woman who makes a man want to conquer the world for her.'

'She is?'

I thought how odd it was that love could make even an intelligent man like Bartels fall back upon platitudes, clichés, and worn-out phrases to express his feelings.

'When I marry Lorna, I shall insist upon a better position in the firm. Something at head office. By God, I've earned it. And I shall demand it.'

'You will? Supposing they don't give it to you?'

'I'll make them give it to me.'

130

'Splendid.'

'There's no reason why I should not be a Director one day.'

'None at all. There is no reason at all why you should not be a Director. I hope you will be. I think you probably will be, before you have finished.'

It was one of those broadly reassuring things which one says to failures. With men who are likely to succeed, you can afford to discuss the probabilities and chances: you can't do that with failures.

The idea that Bartels would ever become one of the heads of the firm was, of course, laughable. He was a failure on the road; he had neither the organizing ability nor the assertiveness to force his way to the top.

The likelihood that the diffident and reserved Bartels could even compel his firm to give him a better job seemed small enough to me. I reckoned that it was about all he could do to hold his position at all. But my words elated him.

'Is that your honest opinion?' he asked. His eyes shone, and the lines and the shadows seemed to disappear.

'Of course it is.'

'If I succeed, it will be entirely due to Lorna's influence.'

'So you suggested before.'

'She makes me feel that I'm pretty good at my job.'

'So you are, I expect,' I said mildly.

My fit of jealousy had departed. I watched his thin figure walking along the narrow track in front of me, the wind ruffling the absurd patch of hair on the crown of his head, and I did not begrudge him his mood of buoyancy.

'You'll have to come and stay a lot with Lorna and me, when we're married,' he said over his shoulder.

I almost laughed out loud. 'That's very kind of you, Barty. I shall enjoy it. When are you thinking of telling Beatrice?'

'Oh, one of these days,' he said vaguely. 'Some time when the moment is ripe.'

He walked along in silence for a few moments. The dog Brutus, beginning to tire a little now, was walking at his heels, indifferent to the possibilities which the hedges offered him.

'There's something I've been wanting to tell you,' said Bartels suddenly. We had come to a gate, and were looking over it, smoking our pipes. The dog, glad of the rest, had flopped down on the ground.

'Go ahead,' I said absently.

'Well, I just want to say how much it has meant to me to have your friendship at this time. That's all.'

'It's nothing,' I said. I couldn't look at him.

'It may be nothing to you, but it's made all the difference to me.'

'I haven't done anything,' I replied uneasily. 'You'd have been all right without me.'

But he shook his head.

'I sometimes wonder whether I could go through with it without having somebody to talk to, I think I might even have given it all up by now.'

For a moment I had a fleeting feeling as though a hand had gripped my heart.

'I should think it's time we went back,' I said, and turned away from the gate.

*

It was after lunch that the dog Brutus died.

The circumstances were as follows.

Bartels and I returned with the dog from our walk. Beatrice had finished the simple household work which she did at week-ends, and the cooking was well under way. She had laid out a tray of drinks in the drawing room, and was reading the papers when we arrived back.

We helped ourselves to drinks, and Bartels and I joined Beatrice in dipping into the newspapers. The dog, tired after his walk, but by no means distressed, lay in his customary place on the rug before the fire. He licked his paws for a few seconds, and then lay content but not asleep.

After a while, Bartels called the dog by name. The animal lifted his heavy head and gazed with his half-blind eyes in the direction of Bartels' voice. He moved his tail slightly, lazily, but made no effort to get up.

Bartels called him again, and this time he got to his feet and walked slowly over to the chair where Bartels sat. He put his head on Bartels' knee, and Barty fondled him, scratching him behind the ears, and stroking his muzzle with his forefinger.

Once, Bartels bent down and rubbed the side of his face against the side of the dog's head. Beatrice made some remark about the dog having grown up with their marriage, because they had bought him as a puppy shortly after the honeymoon. Bartels made no comment about this, but continued to fondle the dog.

Shortly after, Beatrice went out to serve up the lunch.

A little later, we all went into the dining-room, and the dog Brutus followed. When we had finished the meal, Bartels carved a few pieces from the outside of the joint for the dog. Meat being rationed, he did not carve a great deal.

He then went out into the kitchen, saying that he was going to break up some dog biscuits to mix with the meat. About five minutes later, he returned with the plate of food. Beatrice remarked that he had been some time. Had he had any difficulty in finding the biscuits?

Bartels said no, he had found them all right, but made no further comment.

He placed the plate on the floor at the side of the room, under the dresser, and called the dog Brutus. He laid his hand on the dog's back, as he began to eat, kept it there a few seconds, and then returned to his seat at the table.

By this time we were smoking our after-lunch cigarettes. I was talking to Beatrice, but Bartels made no attempt either to join in or to listen. He sat watching the dog eat.

When the dog had finished, I remember seeing it, out of the corner of my eye, move slowly over towards the window. It did not reach the window.

Approximately two yards from the window, it sank slowly to the floor, and rolled on to its side. It sighed once, as though it were tired, and did not move again.

Almost at once, Bartels got up, and went over to the dog, and a few seconds later said, in a funny kind of voice:

'I think poor old Brutus has died.'

Beatrice gave a little cry, and put her hand to her mouth, but she did not rise from the table. I joined Bartels with the dog, and confirmed what he had said.

Bartels remained on one knee, his right hand still on the dog's heart, his eyes fixed upon Beatrice. He said:

'He's dead all right. Quickly, and without pain. That is a good way to go out; no struggles, no fears, no gasps. He just went to sleep.'

Beatrice had risen, and came over and joined us. She was biting the knuckles on her right hand. She looked down on the dog. Her eyes grew moist but she did not cry. She said :

'Poor old Brutus! The house won't be the same without him. Still he didn't suffer.'

I remember now noting the strange, unblinking stare which Bartels gave Beatrice, but I thought nothing of it at the time. I heard him say:

'No, that's the point. There was no suffering. None at all. He had to die some time. So have we all. A few days or months or years sooner or later make no difference. It's not when you die that matters. It's how.'

134

I recalled he had said that once before, all those years ago at the château. But I attached no importance to it.

We buried the dog in a grassy bank at the bottom of the garden, having first wrapped him in an old Army blanket, Beatrice said she would buy a stone with the dog's name on it. Bartels shrugged slightly, and said:

'If you like. But when we leave here – when we're gone – it'll only be a matter of time before the stone disappears too.'

He had a curious sense of the inevitability of oblivion.

*

I said that I had an engagement in London, and I left them that evening, Beatrice and Bartels, together, each to their own thoughts, and actions. I never saw them together again.

Just before I left, an unpleasant little incident occurred. Beatrice was mending some undergarment or other, and Bartels, at the other side of the fire, had been reading; but now he had laid his book on his lap, and was gazing over at Beatrice, apparently deep in thought.

Near the wall was a side table, and above it a landscape in oils, framed in an old-fashioned, heavy, carved frame. After a while Bartels glanced up at the picture, saw that it was not hanging quite straight, and got up to adjust it.

He placed his open book on the side table, and moved the frame. When he moved it, a large, hairy moth which must have gone behind the picture to die in seclusion and warmth the previous autumn, dropped down with a tiny thud upon the open pages of the book.

Bartels made a curious little noise, half gasp, half groan, and shrank back. His face had flushed pink with shock; he stood staring at the dead insect, not daring to approach it.

Beatrice quickly put her mending down, and went over

to the side table, and picked the moth up by its wings. She walked to the fire.

'Not in the fire!' muttered Bartels, but he was too late.

The dead moth hit the embers at one side, and a small flame shot up, flickered for the space of a second, and died down. Bartels had swung round, as I recalled he had swung round before, when a live butterfly had fluttered into the grate at the château.

'Why not in the fire?' asked Beatrice. 'It was dead, wasn't it?'

Dear, practical, dutiful Beatrice!

She went out into the kitchen. Shortly afterwards, I followed her to say good-bye. She was rolling some pieces of filleted fish in breadcrumbs, and looked up at me and said sadly:

'See how he needs me?'

That was my last chance. I did not take it.

On the contrary, I said in those sad, regretful tones I know so well how to adopt: 'He needs you all right. Yes, he certainly needs you.'

Then I kissed her on the cheek.

I went out leaving her alone in the cottage with Bartels.

*

The remainder of the evening was for me a mad rush, a happy whirl of laughter, and food and wine and fast driving.

I drove up to Lorna's cottage and braked the car violently and blew three long blasts on the horn, and leaped out and rang the bell incessantly.

She came to the door.

'Why, hello,' Lorna said. 'What's the uproar about? Are you on fire, or –'

I did not let her finish. I grabbed her by the hand, and pulled her into the house, and slammed the door.

'Come on!' I cried. 'Come on, throw some town clothes on, and get cracking. We're going up to town, to celebrate!'

'Celebrate what, for heaven's sake?' she said, and laughed.

'We'll decide that on the way. Come on, girl, dash up and change into something that isn't evening dress. Let no time be wasted, Lorna Dickson; this is no night for a girl to be on her own in a house in the country!'

'What's special about tonight?' she asked, as I pushed her towards the stairs.

'Nothing's special about tonight. No beautiful girl should ever be alone at night. 'Tisn't safe. Go on. Up you go!'

'But what are we going to do?' she protested.

'One, dash up to London, and have a quick drink and a smoked salmon sandwich. Two, dash in and see a revue, or what's left of it by the time we get there. Three, dash out of the revue, and have some supper and see a cabaret. Four, dash down here again. O.K.?'

'But you can't drive me all the way home again!'

'Who can't?'

'You can't. You won't get home till about four in the morning.'

'That's right,' I said happily. 'That's quite right. Now go and change, and stop arguing.'

She hesitated. Then she turned and ran lightly up the stairs.

'I'll be ten minutes,' she said over her shoulder.

'Too long,' I called after her. 'Cut it down to seven. The horses will get cold.'

She put her head over the banisters. 'If the coachman wants a drink, he can help himself.'

'The coachman will.'

That is one of the memories I shall always retain of

Lorna: her head over the banisters, her grey-blue eyes dancing with the fun of unexpected pleasure.

Loneliness on her part, rush tactics on my part: that's what I had gambled on. I was giving her no chance to wonder if Bartels would mind; no chance to wonder anything at all, if it comes to that.

I did well that evening.

I suppose it was the first expensive evening out she had enjoyed for a very long time. Bartels had certainly insufficient money to do what Lorna and I did that evening. It was laughter all the way, except towards the end of the drive home.

We had turned off the Kingston By-pass, and driven through Esher, and had just turned the sharp bend beyond Esher, when I asked Lorna if she would care to come out again the following week and see another show.

She said nothing, but it was easy enough to guess what she was thinking. So I said it for her:

'I don't suppose Barty would mind.'

'He might be a little – envious. He is such a generous chap, but of course he can't afford evenings like this. And I wouldn't want him to. I think he might be a bit hurt, you know.'

I accelerated and passed a lorry, then dropped speed to an easy forty-five.

'I am not quite sure whether Barty has the right to feel hurt,' I said flatly.

'Meaning?'

'You know as well as I do, Lorna.'

'Yes,' she said softly. Then again: 'Yes.'

Her hand was lying on the seat beside me. I placed my left hand over it, and said: 'You know, my dear, Barty is a terrific romantic. He is always – looking for perfection.'

I gave her hand the merest suggestion of pressure, and replaced my own on the wheel.

'Always looking for it? Do I gather that you are trying to tell me that I am not the result of his first search?'

I shook my head. 'I don't know. Perhaps. Perhaps not. If I knew, I wouldn't tell you. It's none of my business. It's no concern of mine.'

Lorna remained quiet. She had not removed her hand from the seat, but I let it lie there, while I played my last important card.

'Besides,' I said casually, 'he will have to consider the effect of anything he may do upon Beatrice's health.'

I saw Lorna look at me suddenly, but I kept my eyes on the road ahead.

'Her health?'

'Yes.'

'What's wrong with her health? Barty never told me there was anything the matter with her health.'

Poor Lorna! I could guess how the icy fingers of doubt and fear were beginning to grip her by the throat. I longed to stop the car and take her in my arms and comfort her. There was nothing wrong with Beatrice's health, of course. Fundamentally, she was as sound as a bell, though once she had had slight palpitations of the heart through taking too many aspirins.

'I don't think,' I said carefully, 'that her heart is as strong as it could be. Nothing serious,' I added hastily, for if you wish to add an air of truth to a statement it is as well to soft-pedal it.

Then it sounds plausible. Suckers believe it.

'I see,' said Lorna slowly. 'I didn't know that. I didn't know. He never told me that.'

'Oh, didn't he?' I answered. 'He probably didn't think it necessary. It's nothing serious, you know.'

After a while, as she said nothing, I said:

'On the whole, I would rather you didn't mention it to Barty. He might think I was interfering.'

'I think I must mention it. It makes a difference.'

'I wouldn't like to quarrel with him, Lorna. We've been friends since boyhood. I rather wish I hadn't told you now. But I thought you knew, of course.'

She thought for a few moments. 'All right,' she said at length. 'I won't mention it. Thank you for telling me.'

When I dropped her at her home, she asked me in for a final drink. But I declined. I said good-bye to her on the doorstep.

She was smoking a cigarette. I said to her: 'May I have that cigarette you're smoking?'

'If you wish. Why?'

'Because it has touched your lips,' I said.

Corny, of course. I had heard a Swede say it once in Stockholm.

Still, it worked. She smiled gently, and held it out. I took it and put it to my own lips, and touched my hat with a semi-military salute and turned away and climbed into my car and drove off. It had been a most satisfactory evening, and I felt cheerful all the way back.

Poor old Bartels! It was like taking candy from a child. Easy, dead easy, I thought.

Chapter 13

IT was twilight now, but the air remained hot and still in the woods above the château. So still, that I could hear movements in the house, and even the plop as a frog dived off the side of the moat into the water.

There was an occasional rustle in the woods around me, and once or twice a whirring of wings, ending in a flutter at tree-top level, as a belated pigeon arrived to roost. Once, too, I heard a thin, shrill squeal, which ended abruptly as the victim died.

A black-and-white cat came softly down a path, paused when it saw me, and stood stock still, and then turned off swiftly and silently into the undergrowth.

Across the moat, in the château, a figure moved in the drawing-room, and oil lamps were lit, and I saw it was a woman, probably a village woman who helped in the house. Doubtless she was expecting the Americans shortly to return.

In my day, there would have been dancing now.

I saw the room filled with young people in evening dress. Slow-moving old Hans, again, dancing with Mary, the American; big Norwegian Rolf dancing with little blonde Paulette, a daughter of the house; Bob, from Bradford, talking about money with Freddie the bank clerk in a corner. And Ingrid, dressed in her blue-grey dress, sitting on a sofa by herself, her dress matching her eyes, her soft brown hair outlined against the cream walls. Ingrid whom I had lost through my own sad folly. Ingrid, my first love.

I heard the gramophone playing 'My Blue Heaven'. Our tune, we called it. So strong was the image which I formed that I half rose from the log upon which I was sitting, to go to her and say 'May I dance?' And lead her on to the floor, and feel her soft hand in mine, and whisper: 'Our tune, darling'.

I felt the gentle pressure of her hand, and saw the misty light in her eyes, and heard her say: 'I'm glad you asked me in time. Before anybody else.'

I looked for Bartels, but he was not there. Not there any longer. Not on the terrace, either. Nor in his bedroom.

'Bartels!' I whispered in the silence of the wood. 'Barty, where are you, old cock?'

But though the picture was becoming clearer in some respects, in others the present was mingling with the past.

Therefore it was natural that 26 February was suddenly upon me, and as my heart beat faster, Bartels should no longer be there; not at the château, where he and I were happy together.

For I killed Philip Bartels, and I don't regret it, either. At least, I don't think I do.

Chapter 14

WINTER or summer, Beatrice woke early, and would lie in bed thinking or reading until about 7.15. Then she would get up and make the early morning tea, and wait impatiently until she heard, first the newspapers arrive, and after that the letters.

In the early days of her marriage she had tried without success to engage Bartels in conversation with her; she would read items from the newspaper, or from letters, express her opinions in her own forthright way, and await his response.

After a while, she gave it up as a bad job.

Bartels would lie half asleep, allowing his cup of tea to grow cold upon the bedside table; occasionally, if he could not avoid it, he would make a monosyllabic reply and then fall half asleep again.

But on the morning of 26 February, he was awake before Beatrice.

For a while he lay in the darkness of that winter's morning, not moving for fear of awakening her, thinking over what he would do, and, in particular, how he would do it.

It is customary among people of a certain school of thought to say that all murderers must be mentally unbalanced to a greater or lesser degree; poor fellows who are in need of hospital treatment rather than punishment.

I do not consider myself at all unbalanced, and I am quite sure that on the morning of 26 February, Bartels was as sane and cool-brained as anybody else. He had a slightly neurotic fear of moths, dead or alive, and he suffered from a fear of confined spaces, but that is all; and there is not the shadow of a doubt that Philip Bartels came to the decision he did because he was brought up among relations who were so occupied with their own curious interests that they could spare no time to give him the love he needed.

Beatrice could not give it to him; Lorna could. So to Bartels, unable to inflict suffering upon man or woman or beast, there was only one possible way out. The only point he had not decided yet was how exactly he would do it.

He lay in bed thinking, quite calm now, because to a man like Bartels turmoil comes from indecision. He glanced at the luminous dial of his watch, and saw that the time was nearly seven o'clock. He reached up and switched on the light above his bed, and glanced across at Beatrice.

She lay sleeping quite peacefully. He thought dispassionately that this was possibly the last morning when he would see her thus, and he tried to arouse within himself some spark of sentiment.

But the only thoughts that came to his mind were that some day she would have to die, that for her the prolongation of life, perhaps into the feebleness and decay of old age, held no advantages in the long run. For Beatrice to fall asleep, without fear and in the bloom of life, involved no hardship for her.

The alternative for her, as he saw it, was to suffer the loneliness and humiliations of the abandoned wife; he was too fond of her to allow that to happen.

So his thoughts ran, while Beatrice slept on.

At seven o'clock he got up, moving quietly and with stealth, and went into the kitchen and made the early morning tea. He brought the little tray back, and set it on the table by the side of her bed, and gently shook her.

She stirred, and rubbed her eyes and looked at him. Her red hair lay spread out on the pillow. She was wearing a low-cut green nightdress, and the flesh of her arms glowed pink in the light from his bedhead.

She looked young and child-like, tousled with sleep. He thought she looked, indeed, rather beautiful, noting the fact in an unemotional way, and glad that the kind of protective emotional covering which he had assumed prevented the fact from touching his heart.

'Barty? What's the matter?'

He smiled. 'Nothing's the matter. I just thought I would get the tea, for a change. A kind of treat for you.'

'Good heavens. How nice of you, my dear.'

'Miracles never cease, do they?'

He smiled back at her, and poured out two cups of tea. Beatrice sat up in bed, and took her cup and began to sip it.

'You look rather lovely, you know.'

'Thank you, Barty. Praise indeed.'

'Like one of those advertisements you see in magazines. Drink a cup of Slumbo and get eight hours' sleep and be a beauty like me.'

He talked to her for a while, about this and that, for he knew she liked to chat in the early morning, and he was particularly anxious that she should enjoy herself that morning.

After a while, he heard the rustle of the morning papers being thrust through the letter-box. He went out to fetch them, and when he returned he handed one to Beatrice, and opened one himself, sitting on the side of her bed.

For two or three minutes he sat reading and smoking. Then, his cigarette finished, he reached forward to extinguish it in the ash-tray on the table by the side of Beatrice's bed. As he did so, he noticed the bottle of indigestion powder, and the glass on a saucer, and the teaspoon.

He straightened himself, and stared at the bottle. It was nearly empty. Slowly and carefully he began to think round the idea which had occurred to him, much as a cat will peer and cautiously sniff at a plate of food suddenly presented to it.

'Nothing in the paper,' said Beatrice, continuing to read it just the same. She yawned.

Bartels said nothing. He was trying to remember two things. One was how big a dose Beatrice took of the powder, and the other was how often she took it when she had her periodic bouts of mild digestive trouble.

He reckoned there were about four teaspoonsful left in the bottle, and as far as he could recall, having once or twice mixed it for her, she took two teaspoonsful at a time.

Altrapeine was tasteless. That is what the medical book had said. So was the medicine Beatrice took. But was altrapeine really tasteless, or was it a comparative term?

He remembered the dog Brutus. The dog had taken it without trouble. But in that case the powder had been embedded into the meat, and when it came to meat the dog wolfed each piece almost without biting it. It was hardly a fair test.

Supposing he put double the necessary quantity into the bottle, since there were two doses of powder left, and supposing he did not mix the two powders evenly, so that Beatrice took a dose of almost pure altrapeine, would she notice it?

It would be too late, of course, because she always gulped her medicine down, but if she noticed a strange taste – and she had an extraordinarily delicate palate – and then began to lose consciousness, she would be afraid.

She would not suspect him, but she would be afraid. She would think, in the seconds before she died, that the chemist had made a mistake: one read about such mistakes. She would die in fear.

He remembered her fear when she had had her slight attack of palpitations. Her first worried little remark, early one morning: 'I feel funny, Barty. I wish I hadn't taken those aspirins.' And a few minutes later, the piteous little cry of real alarm: 'Barty, I do feel queer; my heart's beating terribly quickly, and I can't seem to get my breath.'

He had calmed her down, only to hear her call out again, a few moments later. She had rushed to the window and flung it open, and gulped down the air, and turned and clung to him with terror in her eyes, and cried: 'Barty, Barty!' and then again, 'Barty, Barty!'

Then, while he telephoned the doctor, she had gone and put her head under a cold-water tap, and had kept moving about the flat, always with fear in her eyes, crying, 'I think I'm better if I keep moving! I seem to be better if I keep moving!'

It had been nothing serious, of course. She had simply knocked off aspirins and taken to phenacetin tablets instead, and had never had an attack since. Her heart was as sound as a bell.

But he remembered how he thought, in agony of mind: 'Not this way, dear God, not by death. Oh, God, don't give me my freedom through her death!'

It had changed since then. Now he not only desired her death: he was plotting it. Now it was freedom by death, yes, but not freedom by death *and fear*. Not that. He would wait a week, a month, a year, rather than that.

He lifted the tea-pot and looked at Beatrice.

'Care for another cup?' he asked.

'Yes, please. Not quite so much sugar this time, please.'

Beatrice answered without looking up from her paper. She was lying back smoking and reading. Soon, as Bartels knew, she would put down her paper and start talking about her plans for the day.

'Been having indigestion again?' he asked. 'I see you've been taking your stuff.'

'Oh, nothing much. I've had one or two twinges in the night lately. That's all.'

'How often do you take the stuff?'

Beatrice had a habit of becoming so deeply immersed in her reading that she was unable to hear questions put to her. So it was now. She did not answer.

'How often do you take it?' said Bartels again, more loudly. 'Twice a day? Three times?'

Beatrice leaned over and extinguished her cigarette in the tray. 'Oh, no. I'm just taking it before I go to bed for a few days. I'll have to get some more.'

'I'll get it for you,' said Bartels.

'I've got enough to last tonight and tomorrow.'

'I'll get some today,' said Bartels dully.

'Oh, don't bother, Barty. There's no hurry.'

'I'll get it for you today,' said Bartels again. 'I've got to go to the chemist anyway to get some blades.'

He heard the postman's knock, and went out and fetched the letters. There was nothing of interest, except a letter from a cousin of Beatrice's saying her sister had had a baby. It was strange that they had never had a child, Beatrice and himself. The doctors could find no reason for it. He wondered if a child would have made any difference, and thought it probably would have done. Strange, then, that a hidden physical defect, some small maladjustment, accidental, invisible, inherited, could make so much difference to three people: could cause a man, indeed, to risk the hangman's noose.

He had the information he wished now. She was taking the powder once a day, before going to bed; and she was taking about two teaspoonsful, as he had surmised.

'I think I'll have my bath,' he said, and went out.

He passed the wardrobe where his suits were hanging. It was in the breast pocket of the oldest one, the one he

148

rarely wore, that the bottle of altrapeine was secreted. It was quite safe there. Beatrice hardly ever went to his wardrobe, and if she did, while he was having his bath, she would have no cause to search in the pockets of that old and dilapidated suit.

Bartels shaved and bathed, slowly, taking his time, and thinking out his next move.

He was still quite calm. Later, his nerves were to cause him trouble. But not yet. He was still enjoying the relief which comes from taking a decision after a period of mental struggle.

During the day, he would have to buy a bottle of Beatrice's medicine.

This, when he returned and found Beatrice no longer alive, he would substitute for the one which had contained the poison. He paused in the act of cleaning his teeth: strange how he baulked at the word 'dead'. 'Beatrice dead.'

It was hard to imagine that forceful and well-organized woman dead. All life stilled, all plans cut short. It seemed utterly impossible.

He glanced at his wrist watch on the shelf above the handbasin. It was nearly 8 a.m. She usually went to bed at 11 p.m.

So in fifteen hours Beatrice would be dead. There was no doubt about it now. Even if he wished to do so, he could not call a halt now because he felt irresistibly caught in a moving band of events from which he knew himself to be no longer psychologically able to escape. He had set the machinery going. He couldn't stop it now. It was stronger than him.

He continued to make detailed mental plans.

He would have to empty all the powder out of the new bottle except for about half a teaspoonful; no more and no less, for in case of investigation, he must guard against the possibility that the 'daily help' might comment, however innocent her remarks, upon the fact that a comparatively new bottle of stomach powder stood by Beatrice's bedside. He did not want the attention of the police, or Dr Anderson, to be drawn unduly to that bottle, though it was possible that they might wish to analyse the remains. That would be all right, of course. He did not wish them to search the dustbin, however, for the old one, and he did not wish to have to explain where it was, when they failed to find it.

It was on small points like that, thought Bartels, combing his hair in the bathroom, that a chap could come badly unstuck.

Like all murderers who plan their crimes, he was supremely confident. He couldn't face a dead moth, he was afraid of being locked in a room. He even felt suffocated when a train in which he was travelling passed through a long dark tunnel, unless the compartment was lighted. But he could pit his wits, gamble his life, risk his reputation in the eyes of posterity, against the most efficient police force in the world. Odd, really.

Now he began to consider the question of disposing of the bottle which had contained the poison. Almost at once a number of difficulties occurred to him.

He pictured the scene on his return. In his hand would be the new bottle, the label suitably rubbed to take away its freshness; by the bedside, the old bottle which had contained the altrapeine. He replaces it with the new bottle. Now he is standing there with the other one in his hand. Within a few minutes he must telephone the doctor, who might be on the scene in a quarter of an hour; perhaps less.

Bartels sat down on the edge of the bath and tried to think clearly. You had to guard against the time factor in these things; more, the time factor, *combined with* an unfortunate coincidence, with the unforeseen: the thing which upset your plans and sent you to the gallows. But how could you guard against something which you could not foresee?

He shook his head impatiently. He was getting abstruse. He must confine himself to difficulties which were real. There were enough of them.

Again he visualized the scene, again saw himself standing there with the bottle in his hand: Philip Bartels, with an incriminating article in his hand; and a telephone near by which he would have to use at once; and a doctor who would be arriving at any moment.

But the Philip Bartels he saw wasn't moving. He was standing still, his brain bewildered by the problem. Now fear was forming in his mind; and panic.

He came back to reality with an effort, took a turn up and down the bathroom; then sat down again and compelled his mind to think calmly. He began to analyse the problem, step by step, beginning with the simplest facts.

He had only two places in which to hide the thing: outside the house or inside.

Was it practical to remove the bottle from the house?

No. It was not.

Why? What's wrong with that?

Because a nosy neighbour might see him throwing it in a street refuse-basket, and connect the action with any later development.

But why not take it out of the house and drop it in the Thames or the Serpentine? That's safe, surely?

No, it isn't. It's even more silly.

Oh? Why?

Because, you fool, they would be able to tell very accurately the time at which Beatrice died. If you were seen to arrive after her death, and to leave the house again a few minutes later, and not return for some time, and if you still had not telephoned the doctor, you would be in a spot, wouldn't you? Some of the questions you would have to answer about that little excursion would be a bit difficult, wouldn't they?

But surely the neighbours, if they saw you at all, would later think that you had gone to fetch the doctor personally?

Plain wishful thinking. They might think it, or they might not: supposing a man taking his dog out saw you go out alone and return alone? And he, or somebody else, saw the doctor arrive later, by himself? And the two knew each other, or Dr Anderson knew one or the other, or both, or treated them professionally, or treated their wives or their children, or the whole dam' lot?

Things could leak out that way, couldn't they?

Better not take the bottle out of the house. Not that night, anyway. The following day, yes. But not that night.

So it will have to stay in the house.

Where?

Well, anywhere, really. Anywhere out of the sight of Dr Anderson. In a cupboard in the kitchen, perhaps. Or in a drawer somewhere. A drawer in the writing bureau. That's it. Dr Anderson will sign the death certificate and go, and that will be that: coronary thrombosis, that's what he would diagnose. That's what the medical book said.

Bartels got up from the side of the bath. The problem seemed to be solved. He was about to leave the bathroom when he stopped dead.

But would that be the diagnosis? The phrase in the book ran: 'The circumstances of death are to all intents and purposes similar to those produced by coronary thrombosis.'

To all intents and purposes? What was meant by that? Were there, in certain cases, symptoms which could raise even the smallest doubt? Complexion, for instance; or the age factor?

Supposing Dr Anderson did not at once diagnose thrombosis of the heart? He was a cautious old stick; unhurried, methodical, and pig-headed. A death certificate could be a dangerous thing to a doctor; wrongly given, it could damage his reputation. Bartels, a layman, could say nothing to put the idea of thrombosis into the doctor's head. Anderson would have to come to his own conclusions in the matter.

He wouldn't suspect murder, of course. That was out of the question.

But suicide? What if he suspected suicide?

Bartels, his head pressed against the bathroom door in an effort to concentrate, imagined Dr Anderson leading him into the drawing-room. Imagined him speaking:

'Not entirely satisfied . . . presume your wife had nothing on her mind? . . . No, no, not as far as you are aware . . of course not, of course not, highly improbable . . . nevertheless . . . stresses and strains of modern life . . . terrible wear and tear on the nerves, Mr Bartels . . . odd, unaccountable things do happen . . . case in the paper the other day . . . have to be so careful, you know . . . feel sure you won't mind if . . . another opinion . . . set my mind at rest . . . police surgeon . . . accustomed to things . . . purely a formality, of course . . . headaches might have unduly distressed her . . . possibility that Mrs Bartels did not wish to embarrass you . . . her last thoughts not to create a scandal . . . police surgeon . . . yes, Mr Bartels . . . if you don't mind . . . just use your telephone?'

The police car, black, smoothly purring, sinister, would draw up outside. The police surgeon would come in, accompanied by a sergeant and a constable. Questions, questions, questions.

Your name? Your wife's christian names? Age? All the rest of it.

While the doctors conferred, the sergeant and constable would be talking to you; polite, deferential, formally sympathetic.

Would you have any objections if they just looked around the flat while they were waiting? A search? Oh, no. Just look around. Just in case 'the unfortunate lady may have had a nervous breakdown, sir'.

No, sir. Of course not, sir. Most unlikely, sir.

Nevertheless, if you don't mind, sir.

We won't make the place untidy, sir.

It won't take long, sir.

Perhaps you could do with a cup of tea, sir?

That's right, sir, sit down there, we'll bring you one. You can drink it while we're having a quick look around.

A quick look around. But it would be a search just the same. By experienced, observant men. First the medicine cupboard, of course. Nothing there, nothing of interest there. Then the bedroom: the cupboard in the bedside table, the bottles on the mantelpiece – lotions, perfumes, and the rest. Then the dressing-table, and its drawers. Then the kitchen. Nothing there, either.

Then the drawing-room.

The bureau. The bureau drawers.

Did your wife suffer a lot from indigestion, sir? Did she usually keep her old stomach-powder bottles?

Can you think of any reason why she should keep one among her boxes of writing-paper, sir?

Sniff, sniff. No smell, of course. Nothing suspicious at all. Just the usual small amount of white powder in the bottom of the bottle.

We'd better just take it along, sir. You don't mind, do you, sir?

Altrapeine, that's what the analysis would show. What woman, what normal housewife would think of committing suicide by taking such a comparatively unknown drug as altrapeine? And if his love for Lorna Dickson became known – 'association', the police would call it – what then?

What then, indeed.

For a few moments Bartels found the problem of the disposal of the bottle the same night too baffling to solve. He stood in the bathroom, staring at the locked door, while the idea grew in his mind that he would have to abandon the whole thing.

It was too risky.

There was not only himself to consider. Lorna would be involved. She would certainly be investigated: the police never forgot the Thompson–Bywater case. Word would get round, that was quite certain. It always did. At the best, her business would be ruined, and she would have to leave the district. Start afresh somewhere else, on practically nothing.

'Too risky,' said Bartels softly. 'Too bloody risky.'

Thank heavens he had tried to plan every detail in advance.

Thank God he had had enough imagination to picture every incident which could happen before it happened. Thus Bartels, feeling in his dressing-gown pocket for his lighter to light a cigarette, decided that he would have to give the whole idea up, not only for that night, but perhaps for always. The same problem would always arise.

He lit his cigarette. Human nature being what it is, a very slight feeling of relief came over him; a man's philosophy of life and death may make him indifferent to humane killing, in special conditions, but to risk the long-drawn-out rigmarole of a trial and the scaffold is a different matter.

Circumstances beyond his control were preventing him from carrying out his plan. What the future held he could not tell; he had not had time to think. But for the moment he need do nothing; and because he need do nothing, he felt the tension relax within him. The machine had stopped, and with it the moving band of events.

He replaced the lighter in his pocket. A simple enough action, but important: for there was the solution: his pocket. It was as simple as that, he thought, and at once the burden of events closed in on him again and he saw that there was no further delay open to him.

He could conceal the bottle that had contained the poison in his trousers pocket. Next day he could walk out with it and dispose of it how he wished.

Whatever Dr Anderson thought, whatever the police surgeon thought, if he came to the flat, there could not possibly be enough evidence to justify the police in holding him and searching him.

Arrests in poison cases take some time. There is an autopsy to be performed, motive and opportunity to be proved senior officers and law officers consulted. It all takes time.

Without an arrest there would be no body-search of the suspect. No officer would have the audacity to request him to turn out his pockets for inspection, within an hour or two of his wife's death from a probable attack of coronary thrombosis, without most damning evidence.

Bartels saw the wheels begin to turn again, the machine start, and the moving band slide forward once. There was no escape. He would go forward because he had to do so.

He had committed himself, not in other people's eyes, who might have been prepared to understand, but in the court of his own self-esteem.

He realized now that there was an important side issue to the act which he had planned. He had been a failure in life; he had lacked courage, self-confidence, and that self-assertiveness which is needful for success.

The act of murder which he planned, the proof that he, Philip Bartels, could if necessary beat the police and society, would bring him not only Lorna Dickson, but, in a twisted kind of way, balm to the self-esteem which had been damaged over the years.

If he drew back now, from fear or lack of tenacity, he

was finished for ever in his own eyes. He would have had his supreme test, dark and secret though it was, and he would have failed.

Uneasily, his hand on the door of the bathroom, Bartels for the first time began to question his motives. Hitherto, he had felt sure that they were based upon love for Lorna, pity for her in her loneliness, and an overwhelming desire to save Beatrice from being hurt and distressed.

Now he had glimpsed something else. Something which he had choked back into his subconscious; something mean and slimy; ignoble, based upon vanity and frustration. A desire to equate himself with others who had defeated their fellow men, had had their triumphs in the world of commerce, or art, or sport.

But they had won their victories openly. At the best, he would be the victor on a secret battlefield, a battle darkly fought, in which the only victim would be Beatrice, a woman who trusted him.

He hesitated to open the door, because he knew that once he passed through it he would be committed to act. There would be no turning back. The depression which had descended upon him was the greater because it followed so swiftly upon the heels of his earlier relief.

He heard the voice of Beatrice calling from the bedroom, asking if he had nearly finished with the bathroom. He glanced at his watch. He had been in there over three-quarters of an hour.

Bartels wrenched the door open.

He went along to the bedroom. Beatrice was up, sitting in front of the dressing-table in her dressing-gown, filing her nails. She looked round as he came in.

'You've been a long time, Barty.'

'Have I? Sorry.'

'What on earth have you been doing?'

'Thinking,' said Bartels.

'Well, I wish you would think somewhere else. What were the great thoughts?'

'Nothing much,' said Bartels. 'Just about this and that. By the way, I shan't be in this evening. I've got some ghastly dinner in Colchester with some local wine society. What'll you do?'

Beatrice thought for a moment. 'I'll probably go and see that film at the local. I've been wanting to see it for some time.'

'Don't wait up for me. You know what these things are.'

When Beatrice had gone into the bathroom, he finished dressing, and went to the wardrobe, and found the bottle of altrapeine. He had bound some adhesive tape round the neck and stopper, lest a few grains should leak out, and, in the event of things going wrong, be found on analysis of his pocket dust by the police laboratory.

You couldn't be too careful.

Then, having nothing further to do at the moment, he went to the kitchen and started cooking the breakfast. There were two eggs in the refrigerator. He fried them, and added two rashers of bacon, and two tomatoes. He also fried some bread. When he had finished, he put the food on a dish, and placed it in the oven to keep warm, and made some toast and coffee.

He had finished the toast when Beatrice came into the kitchen, and he helped her to lay the table.

Beatrice enjoyed her meal. She said so.

'Though what we're going to eat for the rest of the week for breakfast, Barty, I don't know.'

Bartels thought: Brutus enjoyed his run along the hedgerows; she's enjoyed her breakfast. Aloud, he said:

'Eat drink and be merry, for tomorrow we may die. Or today, if it comes to that. You never know.'

Beatrice said: 'Don't be so gloomy, Barty.'

'Well, you never know, do you?'

He hated himself for his grisly humour, and was at a loss to understand why he had made the remark.

After breakfast he went to his typewriter to type a letter to his bank manager. When he had finished, he sat listening.

Beatrice was in the kitchen, washing up. He stamped his letter, put it in his pocket, and went into the bedroom and took the bottle of digestive powder, and went along to the kitchen. He put his head round the door.

'As a matter of fact, my own stomach feels a bit upset this morning. I'm going to steal a dose of your powder. if you don't mind. I've got that dam' dinner tonight.'

'Use one of these cups,' said Beatrice. 'It makes the glass so hard to polish.'

'It's all right. I'll use the tooth-mug in the bathroom.' He went into the kitchen, picked up a teaspoon, and went into the bathroom, and closed the door. He locked the door, but before he did so, he opened the window; such was his fear of confined spaces.

He felt curiously aloof and detached, as though he were watching from close at hand the actions of somebody else called Philip Bartels.

It did not seem possible that it was really he who extracted two teaspoonsful of Beatrice's medicine, and threw it into the basin, and carefully rinsed away the scattered grains from the side. That represented the amount he was supposed to have taken.

He examined the amount which remained: as he had guessed, there was enough left for about one dose. Some of this, too, he extracted, to leave room for the altrapeine.

He unscrewed the top of the little bottle holding the altrapeine powder, and poured the whole amount into the palm of his left hand. Then he tipped up the medicine bottle, and added the remains of the digestive powder.

With the handle of the teaspoon, he stirred the two powders together; round and round, occasionally lifting some of the mixture from the bottom and sprinkling it on top. He stood for about two minutes, stirring and lifting, and stirring again.

Purposely, he had added considerably more altrapeine than the maximum fatal dose. He had to allow for the possibility that Beatrice would not entirely empty the bottle. Finally, again using the narrow handle of the spoon, he carefully ladled the mixture into the medicine bottle, and replaced the screw top.

He rinsed out the little aspirin bottle and put it in his trousers pocket, and filled the tooth-mug with water and emptied it, to make it seem as though it had been used. He wetted the appropriate end of the teaspoon, and washed his hands.

It was done now.

The stuff was in the bottle. There was little more to do, at least at the flat. He took the bottle and spoon into the kitchen, wiped the spoon on a teacloth, and replaced it in its proper place. Beatrice was still at the sink.

'Where shall I put the medicine?' he asked.

'Put it by my bed, will you?'

He went into the bedroom and placed it by her bedside, and looked slowly round the room. Then he went into the sitting-room and glanced round there, too. He might as well remember it. It would never be the same again.

He might spend part of one more night there, but that was all. After that he would leave, and stay in a hotel; or go away. That would be better. He would ask for a week or two off, and go away; anywhere, so long as it was not near the flat. Or near Lorna.

He would have to keep away from Lorna for at least a month; possibly more. She would understand, except that, not knowing the circumstances, she would put it down to his delicacy of feelings.

He would not be able to marry her for at least a year. It

would be unwise to show any indecent haste. There again, chaps were inclined to go wrong: indecent haste; tongues wagging; malicious gossip; tales reaching the police; all inaccurate, of course, but perhaps enough to make the police start making inquiries.

Not that they would be likely to get far, at that late date. Still, you couldn't be too careful.

He went into the hall and put on his overcoat and gloves, and picked up his soft brown hat. It was time to be off.

So that was that.

All that remained now was to say good-bye to Beatrice.

He walked down the passage to the kitchen, and went in, and kissed her on the lips, showing neither more nor less warmth than he normally did.

'Bye-bye, darling,' Beatrice said, and turned back to some cutlery she was polishing.

'Bye-bye,' said Bartels; 'take care of yourself.'

'I will,' said Beatrice. 'You, too.'

He turned and walked out of the kitchen, and down the passage, and out of the front door. He closed the front door behind him, and walked down the stairs.

At that moment, what worried him more than anything else was the complete lack of emotion which he felt. Again he seemed to be watching himself, rather than taking part in the scene.

He had expected a wave of emotion to flood him when he said good-bye to Beatrice for the last time. But it didn't happen. He felt unmoved. As though that morning were the same as any other morning. As though, when he returned that evening, Beatrice, as she often was, might still be awake; sitting up in bed reading, waiting for him, waiting to greet him with a cheerful word, and ask him if he wanted a cup of tea.

It didn't seem right to feel as he did: cold, unexcited.

He began to wonder whether, in fact, he was the abnormal, callous brute history would make him out to be if things went wrong.

Up to now, he had told himself that he was actuated by pity. But even though his philosophy about death was genuinely felt, should he not have experienced a tinge of that same pity when he said good-bye to Beatrice?

Maybe he was indeed abnormal, in some way. Maybe the secret thrill of defeating the police system, of raising himself in his own esteem, played a bigger part in the matter than he had realized.

A worried frown creased his forehead as he left the house.

For the first time, he had grave doubts about his actions. He tried to brush them aside.

*

He was working at head office that day; checking his sales record, answering letters, sending out other letters to say that he would be in such-and-such a town on such-and-such a date, and would like to call and present his compliments to this buyer and that. Mapping out itineraries. Writing to hotels booking rooms.

At lunch time, he took an Underground train to Victoria Station, and went up into the main-line station, and paused outside the Boots chemist shop which is near to the station hotel.

He looked through the door.

Several people were standing at the counter waiting to be served. He went in.

Trade was suitably brisk, the assistants serving one customer and passing to the next with hardly a glance at them. Cough drops. Cold mixtures. Purges. Toothpaste. Soap. Goods and money changed hands quickly. He asked for a bottle of the digestive powder.

'Small bottle or large?' asked the assistant.

Bartels thought furiously.

Which? Which size was the correct one? Which? He didn't know. He just had no idea. This was it. Or could be it. The unforeseen. The unexpected thing which drew attention to you. The thing you couldn't guard against.

He pretended not to have heard. 'I beg your pardon?'

'Small bottle or large, sir?'

'Oh. Small, please.'

He would recognize it when he saw it. If it were the wrong size, he would go elsewhere and buy the right size. She took a bottle from a shelf, and he at once saw it was the right size.

'Don't bother to wrap it up.'

He gave her the exact money, and she turned to the till, and to the next customer. He was just one of the many; a nondescript-looking little man in a grey coat and brown hat, wearing spectacles. Nothing there to excite the interest of a young and romantic chemist's assistant.

He took a bus back to Hyde Park Corner, and walked down Piccadilly to the office. Before going in, he had a sandwich and a large whisky in a public-house.

The day wore slowly on.

From time to time, he thought: perhaps she has not waited till this evening. Perhaps she has had an unexpected attack of indigestion and has already taken the dose.

You couldn't tell. She might already be dead.

His heart began to beat faster as he contemplated the possibility: that would be finality, and he, Philip Bartels, traveller in wines, would be a murderer.

Shortly after four o'clock he could stand the suspense no longer. He dialled the number of the flat.

Instead of the ringing tone, he obtained a high-pitched whining tone. He dialled a second time with the same result.

With a sick feeling at the back of his throat he dialled 'O' and spoke to the operator.

The cold, impersonal little voice at the other end of the line asked him to hold on. He heard her test the number herself, and then say:

'I'm sorry, caller, the line is out of order.'

'Can you have it put right at once?' He hesitated. 'It's important,' he began and then stopped. He couldn't afford to make a fuss, to draw attention to himself.

'I'll report it to the engineers' department,' said the girl in her cool voice.

'Thank you,' said Bartels humbly. 'Thank you.'

He replaced the receiver, and sat staring at the instrument. Then he lifted the receiver again and dialled the number of Mrs Doris Stevenson, who lived in the flat opposite. He heard Doris Stevenson's thick treacly voice, and said:

'Mrs Stevenson? This is Philip Bartels. I wonder if you would do me a favour? I've been trying to ring Beatrice, but the line is out of order. I wonder –'

'I'll see if she's in,' interrupted Mrs Stevenson. 'Hold on a minute.'

He pictured her bulky form waddling across to his flat door; ringing; waiting.

After a while she came back.

'I think she must be out, Mr Bartels. Can I give her a message?'

'Could you ask her to ring me? The fact is,' he added carefully, 'I seem to have lost my cheque book. I want to see if it's at home by any chance.'

'She can ring from here,' said Mrs Stevenson. 'I'll certainly let her know.'

Bartels thanked her and rang off.

A secretary called Miss Latimer came into his room to collect some pamphlets. She looked at him, picked up the pamphlets, and said:

'Are you feeling all right, Mr Bartels?'

'Of course I'm feeling all right. Why shouldn't I be?'

'I thought you looked a little pale, that's all.'

God, did he look as bad as that?

'Oh, nonsense,' he said irritably, and instantly regretted it. This was it, this was one of those unforeseeable things against which you could take no precautions.

He felt the blood flushing into his face. He shouldn't have shown irritation, he shouldn't have answered like that. Now she would remember. He had created an incident out of a normal question. Now she would tell others about it. He felt more blood coming into his face, and put his elbows on the table and buried his face in his hands. All he could think of was the phrase: This is it. Apart from that, his brain seemed to have ceased to work properly.

Miss Latimer said nothing, but he knew that she was standing at the door watching him curiously. Finally, when his face was no longer flushed, he looked up at her and smiled.

'I'm sorry I snapped at you, Miss Latimer. The fact is, I feel all right, that is, I haven't got a headache or anything, but I think I'm getting a cold. I keep feeling cold and then hot and sticky.'

'That's a cold all right.'

He smiled again. 'I suppose it must be. I'll take some hot whisky tonight.'

'I'll give you some of my cold pills, Mr Bartels. I've got some in my desk. They're wonderful. Really, they are.'

'Oh, don't bother, though it's very nice of you.'

But she had gone. In three minutes she was back, carrying two tubes of pills. She was a plump, good-natured girl. Full of kindly actions, thought Bartel bitterly.

'You take a red one in the morning, a green one at lunch time, and another red one before you go to bed.'

'I don't really think I need –'

But she would not let him finish. 'My sister had a shocking cold coming on last week, and she took them, and they kind of nipped it in the bud. Went right away, it did. Never came on at all. And Leslie, in the despatch department, he swears by them now. Go on, Mr Bartels, take them.'

He took the pills and thanked her, and offered to pay for them, but she would not let him.

Red pills and green pills. A fine physic for the soul. One in the morning, and one at midday and one at night.

But he had done right to take them. Better take them and seem thankful, rather than have word go around that 'Mr Bartels was looking queer that afternoon. He wouldn't say anything. Kind of snappish he was. But ever so queer he looked. I remember now.'

Better anything than that.

At four-thirty his telephone rang. It was Beatrice.

'Why, hello, Barty!' Beatrice said in surprise. 'Anything the matter? Mrs Stevenson left a note on the door telling me to ring you.'

'No, nothing, What should there be?'

'I just wondered. You don't often ring up during the day, that's all.'

'I only wanted to ask you how your indigestion was. That's all. Anything wrong in that?' The relief he felt was showing itself in mild irascibility. 'I rang you up earlier, but the phone is out of order. Where are you speaking from?'

Beatrice laughed. She sounded pleased and flattered because he had telephoned. 'A call-box, Mrs Stevenson's gone out herself now.'

'Mrs Stevenson rang the bell, but said you were out.'

'I wasn't,' she said. 'As a matter of fact, I heard the bell ring.'

'Why didn't you answer it? I thought you were out,' he said again. He was angry now, and repetitive in his anger.

'I was washing my hair. I had my head in a basin of water, and by the time I had got to the door, she had gone. I was wondering who it was.'

'Is my cheque-book at home?'

'Yes, it's in the bureau.'

'Good. How is your tummy, anyway?'

'The tummy? Oh, it's all right, thank you, darling. I'll take my usual dose tonight, but I don't think I'll take any more. Don't bother to buy any more, Barty.'

'All right, then. I must be off now.'

'To Colchester? I should have thought you would have been on your way by now. You'll be late.'

'Not if I step on it. Bye-bye, Beatrice.'

'Bye-bye, darling.'

He sat back in his chair. Bye-bye, Beatrice. Bye-bye, darling, she had said. He would never speak to her again. It was a sad little ending.

When he was clearing up before leaving the office, he remembered something which turned him sick with fear.

It was something he had overlooked, not one of the unforeseeables; and the fear he experienced was caused by the thought of what might have happened if he had not remembered it, and by the feeling that there might be something else which he had overlooked.

It was one of the most obvious of all traps, and he had nearly fallen into it: he, who thought he had planned this business so cleverly. He writhed at his own incompetence.

Fingerprints! The thing which the veriest amateur remembers! On the new bottle, the bottle with which he would replace the poison bottle, there would be his own prints. But there would not be a single print from the fingers of the woman who was supposed to have been taking the medicine: plenty of Philip Bartels' fingerprints, and none of Beatrice's.

He stared unseeingly through the office window.

He could rectify that, but the thought of what he would have to do increased his sick feeling: the thought of taking the dead hands of Beatrice and pressing her fingers to the bottle, the fingers of the right hand on to the top of the bottle, and the fingers of the left hand around the bottle.

'I can't do it,' he whispered. 'I just can't do it.'

A voice whispered back inside his head: 'Beaten by a little thing like that? No wonder you're a failure.'

Bartels sighed, and knew he would have to do it after all.

Chapter 15

BARTELS had no intention of going to Colchester, and no dinner appointment even if he had gone there. But he knew he had to be out of the flat when Beatrice died: he knew some of the limitations of his own character, and faced them.

He knew that, if he stayed, there was that within him which would make him cry out at the last moment : 'No! Don't drink it!' And under some pretext or other snatch the glass from her hand.

He could watch Brutus die. His philosophy, such as it was, had enabled him so far to contemplate the death of Beatrice without undue emotion except in so far as his personal safety was concerned. But there he stopped. The theories and logic broke down. He could justify the act, but he could not watch the results.

Therefore he had to be away from the flat until 11.30 or midnight. He did not wish to be with people to whom he was largely indifferent, but with Lorna, who loved him and who would unknowingly give him the strength to tide over the hour between 10.30 and 11.30.

So he took the road out of London, the Kingston By-pass, and navigated the five traffic roundabouts which led to Thatchley, and recalled how he used to think of them, once, as the Five Roundabouts to Heaven.

He assured himself that he still did, of course, and that the depression which was weighing him down was due to nothing more than the nervous tension which the day, not unnaturally, had produced in him.

He left the office promptly at 5.30. The bitter cold of the previous few days had continued. Occasional flurries of snow were still falling, and the headlights of the continual stream of cars approaching London dazzled him, so that he was compelled to drive slowly and with care.

The whine of the windscreen wiper, an old-fashioned type, added to his depression. The thing squeaked protestingly on the windscreen, and twice the blade faltered and stopped while the mechanism continued to moan ineffecually.

Once, he spoke out loud, above the noise of the engine and of the windscreen wiper and of the wind: 'It's not when you die that matters – it's how. What are a few years more or less in the infinite, limitless realm of Time?'

And once he said: 'It's better this way. It's better for her to avoid the suffering and the loneliness. It's a form of mercy murder, that's all. Mercy killing is almost condoned by society for physical suffering, why not for mental? Why not for the suffering of the mind and spirit?' It was his old argument, brought out to comfort him on his way.

But were they Five Roundabouts to Heaven? Or did they lead to Hell? They did, if the Scriptures were right. But the Scriptures, the Ten Commandments, the thou-shalt-not-kills and thou-shalt-not-covets, were a mere set of simple rules to maintain order among a wandering desert tribe. Moses was an old fraud who had gone up into a mountain and come down again claiming Divine inspiration for some rule-of-thumb laws which he had thought up in his goat-skin tent.

Did God exist? If He did, what was He thinking now of him, of Philip Bartels, scurrying through the snow and the traffic because he, Philip Bartels, needed the company of a woman to prevent him thinking too much about a deed so logical, a deed so humane?

If the deed were so humane, did he need distractions for his thoughts? A deed, a deed, distractions from a deed. And this foul deed shall smell above the earth, that's what he had recited at school. Smell above the earth. With carrion men groaning for burial. Cassius, he had been. Not Royal Caesar. But yesterday the word of Caesar might have stood against the world.

But yesterday the word of Philip Bartels might have stood against nothing. Nor tomorrow. Nor the day after. Did he expect Lorna to make a man out of him? Could he expect that? And one laughed in his sleep, and one cried 'Murder'; but that was in Macbeth, a play about another murderer.

Another? Wherefore *another*? One cried 'God bless us', and 'Amen' the other. Duncan's guards. I could not say 'Amen' when they did say 'God bless us'. Wherefore could I not pronounce 'Amen'? I had most need of blessing. Wherefore said I *another* murderer? Macbeth and Caesar. The killer, the victim.

He had been Cassius, the killer, but that was at school. Cassius at school; and would Beatrice's spirit, ranging for revenge, come hot from – heaven, if there were a heaven? And with Ate by her side cry, 'Havoc, and let loose the dogs of war'? The windscreen wiper stuck again, but the blade turned upon its axis, saying: Havoc-havoc-havoc.

Bartels drew the car in to the side of the road until the shivering in his limbs had died away. Perhaps he was, in fact, getting a cold. Perhaps, all unknowingly, he had told Miss Latimer the truth. If he had caught a chill, if he were confined to his bed, how would that affect things?

Not at all, except that he would have to nurse himself. Alone. In some cheap hotel bedroom. He was in Cobham now, and caught sight of a hotel, and eased the car along to it, and went in and had a large whisky and soda.

He felt so much better that he ordered another. He had time for it, if he drank it quickly, as he had done the first one.

He raised the glass and was about to do so, when he paused.

He must not drink it quickly. He must drink it slowly, unconcernedly. He had already acted unwisely in ordering a second large one, in drinking the first so hurriedly.

He must linger over this one, as though he had all the time in the world, and not a care in the world, because if things, somehow, went wrong, and if his photograph were to be published in the papers, and if the barman saw it – what then? He imagined how it would go in Court.

'And you were on duty at the bar of your hotel on 26 February, is that right?'

'That's right, sir.'

'How do you manage to recall the date so accurately?'

'Because it was so bitter cold that night, sir.'

'And I believe that while you were on duty, somebody came in and ordered a whisky and soda, a large one. Do you see that person anywhere in Court?'

'Yes, sir.'

'Well, point him out to the jury, please.'

'It was him. In the dock.'

'How do you manage to remember him so well?'

'I remember thinking that he had a very wide mouth for his size, sir. And wore specs with gold side-pieces. Rather old-fashioned specs, I thought. Spectacles, I should say.'

'Remember anything else about him?'

'He looked pale, sir.'

'He looked pale, did he? Anything else?'

'Well, kind of hot and bothered.'

'What exactly do you mean by kind of hot and bothered? Try to be a little more precise for the jury, will you?'

'Well, kind of upset. As though he was afraid.'

'Agitated and distressed, would you say?'

'Yes, sir.'

'What made you think that, apart from him looking pale?'

'Well, sir, he ordered a double whisky, and drank it very fast. kind of gulped it down. And then he ordered another, and gulped that down, too, and went straight out. I could understand him gulping the first one, sir, owing to the weather and so on. But I remember thinking it a bit odd about the second. 'That's queer,' I said, 'two doubles like that, quick as a flash.' That's why I remember him, really. Whisky costing what it does, most gentlemen like to linger over it a bit.'

'So you would definitely say that he looked agitated and distressed?'

'Yes, sir, I would.'

'Thank you.'

Then Counsel for the defence, of course. Twisting and turning and wriggling. Trying to make out it was quite normal for a man to look pale on a cold night and gulp down two large, expensive, double whiskies, in about three minutes, and go out into the cold again. All that sort of nonsense.

Quibbling and quibbling about identification. Haven't you seen lots of men with large mouths? Is it so rare that you see a man with spectacles like that? You admit you have seen his picture in the papers? So you didn't have much trouble about picking him out in Court, did you? You admit that?

You admit this, you admit that, you admit the other.

Yes sir. No, sir. Three bags full, sir.

And on and on and on.

So he must drink it slowly. Very slowly, when all the time he wanted to be with Lorna. To find strength in her steady blue-grey eyes, tranquillity in gazing at her brow and at her calm, rather squarely-cut jaw.

But he must be careful. First, Miss Latimer: he had snapped at Miss Latimer. Now, he had nearly attracted attention by drinking too much too quickly. Miss Latimer in Court, plump and bewildered, the perkiness knocked out of her, awed by her surroundings:

'Well, sir, he seemed a little upset about something.'

'And why do you think that, Miss Latimer?'

'He kind of snapped at me.'

'And that was unusual?'

'Yes, sir.'

'How unusual?'

'Well, very unusual. He was such a good-tempered man. I've never known him get cross before. Not like that. Snappish, so to speak.'

'Was there anything which made you think he was – not quite himself, shall we say?'

'Well, he looked a bit pale one moment, and hot and red the next. And he put his head in his hands.'

'And how did he explain that away?'

'He said he thought he might have a cold coming. So I gave him some red and green pills.'

'And did the cold develop?'

'No, sir.'

'But that might have been due to the remarkable efficacy of your – ah – little red and green pills?'

Laughter in Court, of course. Ha-ha-ha, very funny. Swiftly silenced by the officials.

Bartels moved over to a chair by the wall. He took out the tube of pills, extracted a few, threw them in the fire. You couldn't be too careful. Miss Latimer, and the barman, one mistake and one near-mistake, in a couple of hours. And the fingerprints. So much to think of, so many of the foreseeables and the unforeseeables.

He took ten minutes to drink his second whisky, and then, while the barman was serving somebody, he went quietly out.

He arrived at Lorna's house in the lane near Thatchley at about seven o'clock. The light was switched on in the porch, offering warmth and shelter from the snow, and from the darkness of the night, and from the black shafts of his thoughts.

Lorna heard the car arrive, and before he could reach the door she had opened it and stood in the porch light to welcome him.

'You must be frozen, Barty.' She smiled affectionately at him, and he took her eagerly in his arms, in the doorway, and kissed her.

'I'm not exactly perspiring in every pore.'

'Come in, I've got a fine blaze of a fire in the sitting-room.'

He took off his coat and hat, and put them on a chair in the hall, and followed her into the sitting-room.

'A drink to warm you up, Barty?' She moved over to the table by the side of the wall.

'Gin and mixed?'

'I'd rather have a whisky and soda, if you can spare it.'

'Of course I can spare it. It's yours, anyway. You bought it.'

Bartels, standing in front of the fire fondling the Corgi's ear, said: 'Don't keep telling me that such few little things as I give you are mine really. They aren't. They're yours, or at the most ours, darling.'

She mixed a gin and Italian for herself and a whisky and soda for Bartels, and brought them over to the fireplace. She gave him his glass and raised her own, and said:

'Well, cheers. God bless us, my dear.'

One cried 'God bless us' and 'Amen' the other. I could not say 'Amen' when they did cry 'God bless us'. Wherefore could I not pronounce 'Amen'? I had most need of blessing. Wherefore must I always think of the guards in Macbeth, thought Bartels. Murdered in their sleep, like Duncan. Beatrice would be murdered just before she would have gone to sleep. He glanced at his watch. Seven-fifteen. Eight-fifteen, nine-fifteen, ten-fifteen, eleven-fifteen. Four hours. Hours and days and years, and what are a few years more or less?

Ten million light years for the light of a star to cross the empty spaces of the night. Ten million more for the light of some star beyond the star to reach that star. The fault, dear Brutus, lies in ourselves not in our stars. The dog, Brutus, he was dead too. Beatrice would be all right, but would he, Philip Bartels?

Beatrice, barefooted, twanging a harp? Not likely!

Beatrice the competent, her red hair aflame in the light of a thousand suns, armed with Delegated Authority, sorting out the Milky Way! That was more like it. Could it be that the slayer was more affected than the slain, the murderer than his victim?

'Are you feeling all right, Barty?'

He wanted to snap back that he was certainly feeling all right, why shouldn't he be feeling all right, what made her think he wasn't feeling all right? But he had learnt his lesson.

'I feel all right thank you,' he replied gently. 'Why?'

'You look a bit pale, that's all.'

'I think I may have caught a little chill. It's nothing.'

He put his arm around her shoulders, and tilted her face up and kissed her.

'You shouldn't have come, if you have got a chill,' said Lorna. 'Not on a night like this.'

'What should I have done?'

'Stayed at home.'

'And not be with you? No, thank you.'

'Well, you'd better take a couple of aspirins before you go to bed.'

What time would he be going to bed? One o'clock? Two o'clock? It all depended. Perhaps three o'clock or four; in that case he would be taking his aspirins with the cup of tea which the sergeant and constable would bring him while they 'looked round the flat' as they'd call it. He didn't know what time he would be going to bed.

'One of the secretaries at the office gave me some red and green pills to take. She says they're very good.'

'Have you taken any?'

He nodded. Even Lorna had to be deceived in a small way. Even for Lorna it was as well to provide a reason why his cold did not develop. Then he realized that this was unnecessary: he would not be seeing Lorna again for a month or so. So he needn't have lied to Lorna. He would never lie to Lorna again, nor to anybody else, once this business was over. He was tired of subterfuge, fed up with intrigue.

He placed his arm round her shoulders and held her more tightly, not kissing her, however, but gazing silently at the carpet, as though trying to draw strength from the tranquillity which for him was one of her most wonderful characteristics.

'Darling Lorna, I do love you so.'

He slid his hand from her shoulders to the side of her head, and pulled her head down so that it lay on his shoulder, and bent down and put his cheek against her brow. Lorna reached up and put her hand on his, and caressed it.

Her hand was soft, her movements gentle, and little by little he felt the agitation within him dying down. Suddenly, she removed his arm, and said:

'Now, young man. I'm going to get the supper.'

'I'll help you.'

He started to follow her to the door, and the Corgi, instinctively guessing that food was being discussed, rose to its feet and pattered after her, too.

'Go and sit by the fire, Barty,' said Lorna. 'Get thoroughly warm. Most of the supper is ready.'

'I'd rather help you, darling.'

'There's nothing you can do, Barty. Really there isn't. The trolley is laid – I thought we'd eat in here, as it's so cold – the soup just needs heating up, and all I've got to do is to throw a little liver and bacon into the pan. The potatoes are cooked. So go and sit down.'

'I'd rather be with you. I would much rather be with you.'

But she pushed him gently from the door, towards the table where the drinks were standing.

'Don't be obstinate. Pour yourself another whisky, a good stiff one, and go and sit by the fire. I won't be ten minutes.'

He watched her go out, and did not dare to insist upon being with her, because that might have seemed unnatural. Tonight he could not afford to appear anything other than composed and normal. He poured out the whisky, sat by the fire, glad that he had not insisted. Tonight was the test of will-power. Once again he felt a curious little thrill which was entirely unconnected with Lorna.

He, Philip Bartels, was in conflict with all the forces of society. That took some doing. That required organization, forethought, nerve, courage. Admittedly, he had hesitated, had had qualms, even some personal fears.

Why not, indeed? What was more natural?

He might not be a very good traveller in wines. In fact, he thought, swallowing some of the whisky, he was frankly a pretty bad salesman. Well, not bad, perhaps, but not very good. One had to face that fact.

But he had won Lorna. And having won her, he had not let circumstances defeat him, as most other men might have done.

No fear! He had gone into action. Decisively. But with care and forethought, mind. Not rashly, committing one blunder after another, as others did. Coolly.

He wondered how many of the smooth gentlemen who disparaged his wines, even declined to see him when he called, would have had the nerve to do what he was doing.

They'd either have run out on Beatrice – a squalid and untidy procedure – or abandoned the whole project. It's all very fine and dandy to sit in an office countering the arguments of wretched commercial travellers. Any fool could do that. But to take on the organized protective forces of the community, that was quite a different thing!

Some people might think he, Bartels, was a bloody fool. A bit of a poor fish. But he wasn't. Not entirely. He was like the iceberg, which only shows a bit of itself on the surface, and he was just about as cool, when the need arose – though normally warm-hearted, mind you, very warm-hearted.

He put the empty glass on a table at his side, and stroked the head of the Corgi, and thought of the dog Brutus lying under the snow at the end of the garden. Brutus wouldn't get his headstone now. Well, what the hell did that matter?

What would become of the cottage?

It would presumably be his. He would sell it, of course. Couldn't live there again. That would be too much. Or he might give it back to Beatrice's parents. As a gesture. They would be upset, of course. But they'd get over it. They had three other children, and anyway they only saw Beatrice two or three times a year.

He heard the squeak of the trolley wheels in the passage, and got up and opened the door.

Rather to his own surprise, he was not very hungry.

'It's your cold coming on,' said Lorna.

'Perhaps,' said Bartels, staring at a little Empire clock on the wall which showed 8.15.

'Maybe,' said Bartels.

It seemed only a few minutes since there had been four hours to go.   Now there were barely three. Or even less. Time passed quickly sometimes.

Chapter 16

Up in the woods above the château an owl hooted, and on the highway I heard the sound of a car.

Not yet, I thought, not yet. Don't let them return yet. Don't let them come swooshing round the drive in their high-powered car, the glaring headlights lighting up the woods; and come tumbling out of the car, laughing and joking after their day out, this one saying how hungry he is, that one calling out for somebody to go mix him the biggest goddam highball ever thought of, and the women calling to the children, and the lamps being lit all over the house, and the sound of snatches of song; and laughter, more laughter.

Nice people, no doubt, gay and generous and big-hearted, but I didn't want them yet. Not just at that moment, when I had almost worked it all out, nearly had the picture clear of the workings of the mind of Philip Bartels, my friend.

The sound of the car drew nearer; then passed, and died away in the distance. I relaxed, thankful. The owl hooted again.

My pipe had gone out long since. I did not bother to relight it.

Chapter 17

IT was about 8.30, and Bartels and Lorna had finished the soup, and were just finishing the liver and bacon, sitting before the fire, the trolley between them, and George the Corgi was looking hopefully from one to the other. Lorna said:

'How is Beatrice?'

Bartels, picking about with his liver and bacon, looked at her in surprise.

'Why?' he asked in an astonished tone.

'Didn't she have palpitations, or something, once?' asked Lorna, breaking a promise.

'Oh, that. Yes, she did, once.' He was about to add: 'Her heart is sound enough, though,' when he stopped himself.

How much did a layman know about palpitations? he wondered. Did a woman like Lorna know that palpitations due to a few too many aspirins, a purely temporary allergy, had no significance at all? Might it not be as well to prepare her in some way for the news about Beatrice?

He toyed with the idea, then cut off a corner of liver and gave it to the Corgi, and watched the dog eat it and look up for more. He put the idea aside. There was no point in trying to be too clever.

Lorna had finished the liver and bacon, and had turned towards the fire. She was peeling an orange, saying nothing, throwing the peel in the fire. Bartels mentally picked up the idea again, turned it round and round, and over. Why not? What harm could it do? One mustn't overdo it, of course. Just toss the sentence out casually.

'Hearts can be a bit tricky,' he said absently, and left it

at that. He was tempted to elaborate, but he resisted the urge, and congratulated himself upon his artistry.

'Yes,' said Lorna, still staring into the fire.

'Cigarette?' Bartels extended his case.

Lorna shook her head silently, began dividing her orange up into segments. The Corgi, seeing nothing further was to be gained in the way of liver, walked to the grate and curled up for a nap.

After a while, Bartels said: 'What's the matter? You're very thoughtful.'

'I've good cause to be.' She looked at him and smiled sadly.

'Why? What's the matter?'

Some premonition of disaster, or the unaccustomed sadness on Lorna Dickson's face, gave Bartels a curious feeling in the pit of the stomach. He shifted uneasily in his chair.

'What's the matter?' he asked for the third time. 'For heaven's sake tell me; don't just sit there.'

'Barty,' she began. 'I don't want you to get the wrong ideas about what I'm going to say – there is no other man who means as much to me as you and never has been since Ronald was killed.'

She paused while Bartels, wide-eyed, still, and unblinking, heard the wild tolling of alarm bells above the crash and surge of breakers on a rocky beach, and above that, louder and louder, the roll of drumbeats, in his breast, his head, every part of his body even to his finger-tips.

Lorna was looking him straight in the face now. Her lips were slightly parted, her serenity was disturbed, but the inner beauty, glimpsed through the grey-blue eyes, was untarnished.

She rose and came and sat on the arm of Bartels' chair, and put her arm round his shoulders, and pressed him against her side.

'Barty, I don't think we can go through with this thing,

dearest. I have given it a lot of thought. I don't think it's fair to Beatrice, and above all, it might be dangerous for her,' she hesitated, groping for the right phrase. 'Above all, I don't think it's even fair to you – or me.'

'Why?' whispered Bartels.

The alarm bells had ceased tolling, the breakers had receded, leaving exposed the jagged black rocks of despair. But the drums were still beating louder and faster than ever.

'Why, Lorna? Why? Lorna, darling Lorna, you can't let me down now. Not at this stage.'

She began to stroke his light brown hair, trying ineffectually to flatten the bits which stood up on the crown of his head.

'Do you wish me to marry you to avoid letting you down? From a sense of duty? Is that what you are suggesting?'

'This is only a passing qualm, Lorna.'

He tried desperately to sound cheerful. 'You'll feel better tomorrow. Come on, let's have a drink! What's yours?'

He tried to get out of the chair, but she gently pushed him back. 'Not now, my dear. This is not a time for drinks. This is the moment for clear thinking and talking.'

He sat back in the chair, then, very still, his eyes staring at the ceiling, pale and drawn, the firelight reflected in the lenses of his spectacles.

'Don't you see?' said Lorna miserably. 'Don't you see? If anything happened to her, we should never forgive ourselves. She would always be between us.'

'Would she?' asked Bartels bitterly. 'Would she really? So they say in books of fiction. She would always be between us. Her shadow would come between us. Our happiness would turn sour. I know, I know, I've read about it. I wonder whether it is true. I doubt it.'

'I, for one, can't risk it.'

The plans, the precautions, the hesitations, the fears, all

were pointless. Beatrice was to die, a sacrificial victim on an altar of failure.

Even if Lorna changed her mind before he left, when she heard that Beatrice was dead she would think that he had taken matters into his own hands, had told her the truth; and that Beatrice had had a heart attack as a result. Lorna would never forgive him or herself.

He heard Lorna say. 'I know what this means to you.' He thought how often people said that, and how little they really knew. He heard her add: 'Believe me, I would like to have married you more than anything. But not this way.'

'Not this way,' he repeated softly.

That's what he had said when Beatrice had her little palpitations and was so scared and unhappy.

Not this way. My freedom, yes, he had said, but not this way, not by her death; and later he had modified it, and said, not by her death in fear or pain.

'Don't let's come to any final decision tonight,' he implored her, but again he thought: What's the use? If Beatrice dies, Lorna will blame me and herself.

'I think it's as hard for me as for you,' said Lorna. 'And I've already come to the decision. I shall feel no different tomorrow.'

Suddenly, she put her arms round him and placed her cheek against his brow, as he had done to her earlier in the evening.

'Oh, my dear, I know it's hard, but try not to take it too badly. Let's see if we can't get through to the end of our lives now without causing too much damage.'

After a while he said, quite simply: 'All right, if that's what you want.' He put her from him, firmly but not roughly, and rose to his feet. 'Mind if I have that drink now?'

Lorna went over to the drink table, poured him out a whisky, and handed him the glass.

'Aren't you drinking?'

She shook her head, and stood by the grate, both hands on the mantelpiece, looking down into the fire. He drank half the whisky without a pause.

'What about us – now?' he asked.

'I think we should break it up,' whispered Lorna. 'Half and half is no good, Barty.'

'All right,' he said, and drank off the remainder of the whisky. 'As you wish.' He replaced the glass on the table.

'Don't you think it better?' asked Lorna, still staring into the fire.

'As you wish,' said Bartels again. 'I am going now. Thank you for your past kindness. Also for tonight's supper.'

Lorna swung round quickly from the mantelpiece.

'Don't let's part like that, Barty, dearest.'

'Like what?'

'In bitterness.'

She made to put her arms round his neck, but he drew back.

'Don't let's part like that, either.'

She let her arms fall to her sides. 'You think I'm beastly, I know, I'm sorry about that. I didn't want that to happen.'

Bartels sighed and shook his head impatiently.

'I think you might have let me know a little earlier, that's all.'

He was beginning to feel the panic rising inside him, in recurring waves; rising and subsiding, then rising again. Provided Beatrice adhered to her plans, he had time to get back. But he had to leave at once to be on the safe side. He had to go, now, without delay.

His emotions were confused, the pain caused by Lorna's decision was anaesthetized by the fear that Beatrice might die for nothing, and the shock of Lorna's words was deadened by the urgent need to get back to London as fast as he could.

Deep down, he was bitter and hurt, but those feelings

were temporarily submerged beneath the turmoil of other emotions. He resented now every minute he had to spend in the house. He glanced at the clock. It was ten past nine. An hour and a half. Less, to be safe.

He moved towards the door. He moved slowly, because the position was in one respect as it had been earlier: he could not afford to act unnaturally.

At the door, he turned. Lorna was standing in the middle of the room, looking after him.

'Let's pretend I'm nipping down to the local to buy a bottle of gin,' he said. 'Let's make it easy, like that.'

His hand was on the door-knob when a thought occurred to him, and he paused, and came back into the room, and stood staring at the carpet, while the blood rushed into his face, as it always did when he was suffering from a sudden shock.

She had a habit of keeping his letters, and he had sent her a great many. He was trying to think quickly, to remember any phrase or phrases he may have written which, if the worst came to the worst, would sound damning in a court of law.

For a few seconds all he could think was: Thompson and Bywaters, Mrs Thompson, Frederick Bywaters, what had she written that had sounded so damning in Court? Glass, it was something to do with glass. 'I have tried the ground glass in his food, but it didn't work,' something like that. Dramatizing herself, some said.

Her letters were found in his sea-chest, or somewhere. Both were hanged. His thoughts raced on. They put a white bag over your head, so that you felt all shut in, suffocating, worse than being in a locked room or a dark tunnel. He'd shout and struggle if they tried to do that to him, and it'd all be sordid and undignified.

A wave of claustrophobia swept over him, so that perspiration broke out on his forehead, and he had to clench his fists and breathe deeply, until, little by little, he could force his thoughts back to the letters he had written to Lorna.

Lorna Dickson stared at him. 'Are you feeling all right, Barty?'

'Yes,' he said. 'Yes, I'm all right. Just let me think for one moment.'

She said nothing, but moved over to the side table and poured out a small glass of brandy. She brought it over to him, but he only said:

'No, no, thank you. Not that. Just let me think clearly, Lorna. Clearly, just for a minute.'

But there was nothing in his letters. He was sure of that. There was no reason why there should be. What could there be? He hardly ever mentioned Beatrice in his letters.

He sought to concentrate his mind more narrowly upon recent letters – letters from Manchester, Bradford, Leeds, the south coast.

What had he written from Manchester, where he had bought the altrapeine? There was a mention of Beatrice in that letter, a reference to a talk with Lorna about telling Beatrice the truth, asking her to release him. It was before he had made up his mind to act differently. Only he hadn't made it as clear as that in the letter.

Then he remembered the words he had used, and the significance of them again sent the blood rushing to his face.

'*About Beatrice,*' he had written, '*I shall arrive at the cottage tomorrow evening. We shall be alone this week-end. A good opportunity to do it.*'

And now he remembered another, an earlier one, written from Cardiff. Some time ago now; but that didn't matter, that didn't matter at all, that merely tended to show how long a time he had been premeditating it all: '*I will spend the first part of the evening with you, my beloved, and from you I*

*will draw the strength to enable me to do that which we both
know has to be done some time.'*

He sat down on the arm of an easy-chair and covered his
face with his hands. Lorna came to his side and put her arm
once more round his shoulders.

'What is it, Barty?'

He put his hands down, and got up and moved to the
mantelpiece, and stood there irresolutely, still trying to
think of other references, still trying to decide what to do.

There was at least one other reference, but he couldn't
exactly recall it, except to remember that he had thanked
her for reassuring him that he would be justified in doing
what he contemplated.

All were references to the talk which at one time he
thought he would have with Beatrice; each and every one,
taken in conjunction with other factors, was enough to
sway the minds of a jury; enough to implicate Lorna as well
as himself.

They hanged Mrs Thompson. What of Lorna? What
chance does 'the other woman' have in cases like this?

Counsel in Court. Bewigged, hard, implacable Counsel.
Hitching up his gown, smiling, self-confident.

'You have, then, members of the jury, ample evidence
that the death of Mrs Bartels was calculated to further the
sordid plans of both the accused.

'You have evidence that Mrs Bartels died from the effects
of a poison which it is extremely difficult to detect, the
symptoms of which, but for the praiseworthy vigilance of
the local practitioner, might easily have been confused with
those indicating coronary thrombosis.

'You have the evidence of the Manchester chemist that a
man, whom he has identified as the prisoner Bartels, bought
altrapeine in his shop, that he had removed his glasses to
make himself less readily identified, and that he signed the
poisons book using the name and address of a perfectly

respectable Leeds business man who bore no resemblance to the prisoner, and has never bought altrapeine in his life.

'And you have those highly significant remarks in his letters to the woman Lorna Dickson: "We shall be alone this week-end. A good opportunity to do it". And again: "From you I will draw the strength to enable me to do that which we both know has to be done some time". Note the words, please: that which *we both know* has to be done. Ample evidence, I submit, that the woman Dickson knew that this horrible crime was going to take place.'

The witness Miss Latimer. The hotel bartender. Agitated and distressed.

And on and on and on.

Nobody would put anything but the most sordid constructions on his love for Lorna. Nobody would believe that it was love and not sensual lust which had prompted the crime.

Bartels swung round from the fire. It was twenty past nine, now. He said abruptly:

'Lorna, my dear, may I have back the letters I wrote to you – now?'

Lorna said: 'Of course you can have them back. But you don't want them tonight, surely?'

'Wouldn't it be better?'

'What do you want to do with them? Burn them, I suppose?'

'It is better for both of us to have them out of the way.'

Lorna smiled faintly. 'You are being very practical, Barty.' She thought for a moment and added: 'Won't you trust me to burn them for you? Or post them to you at your office, if you wish?'

'It's the sort of thing one can forget,' said Bartels, trying to keep his voice steady. 'It might be better if you gave them to me now, Lorna. If you don't mind, that is.'

'My dear, they are all over the place. Some in the bureau, some in the drawer of my dressing-table, all over the place.'

Bartels thought: ten minutes to collect them, or fifteen minutes, or perhaps more. And then no guarantee that he had them all, that he had the important ones. What was the good of it? Better to go now, and drive fast. Already ten minutes had gone by.

'You don't think I'm going to blackmail you with them, do you, Barty?' Lorna spoke jestingly, trying to lift the tension which had settled in the room.

But he answered her seriously. 'No,' he shook his head, 'no, I know you won't do that. No, it's not that at all.'

He couldn't press the matter any further. Apart from the time factor, it would look peculiar. He felt that already he had gone further than he should have done.

He looked at her helplessly, his brown eyes worried behind the old-fashioned spectacles, his hair standing up slightly on the crown of his head. His face, with the wide mouth and thin straight nose, normally sallow, was flushed by the whisky he had drunk, and the heat of the room, and his state of excitement.

'Never mind,' he said slowly. 'Don't let's bother about them tonight.'

'I'll post them to you tomorrow, Barty – to your office, by registered post, marked private and personal, shall I?' She tried to seem brisk and normal.

'No,' said Bartels quickly. 'Don't bother to do that. Burn them, Lorna, tomorrow morning. The whole lot, without fail.'

Lorna nodded. 'As you wish.'

Bartels looked once round the room, and then at Lorna Dickson. She stood under the chandelier, and returned his gaze. For fully a minute they stared at each other, sad-eyed, uncomfortable, not knowing exactly what to say now that the moment had come to part.

Bartels felt little bitterness now. Numbly, through the pain and the eddies of fear in the back of his mind, he realized that this was the end of his search. Whatever happened, there would be no love in his life of the kind of which he had dreamed as a boy, because there never would be and never could be another Lorna.

Watching Lorna, he began to doubt for the first time whether in fact she was, or ever had been, truly in love with him. Else why had she shown comparatively little emotion this evening?

Surely, if one were in love, as he was, you forged ahead irrespective of other people's feelings, ruthlessly, driven on by a fire which nothing could withstand. You cared nothing for anybody, you were prepared to strike, and even to destroy as he had planned to destroy.

That was it, that was the test: you were prepared to destroy. Lorna wouldn't go even half-way with him on that score.

Illogically, he felt irritated at her calm. Childishly, he thought that she might at least pretend to feel more emotion. Petulantly, he thought that greater signs of distress were even his just due.

But he said nothing.

He turned round suddenly, and opened the drawing-room door and went into the hall and put on his coat and hat and gloves, and walked slowly to the front door.

Lorna followed him to the front door, and the Corgi dog, thinking that a walk might be in the offing, was at her heels.

He opened the door and the dog went out. Bartels paused.

'Well, what are you going to do now?' he asked inconsequentially. 'Going to bed?'

She nodded. 'I'm tired.'

He pulled out his cigarette case, and offered her one, and when she refused lit one himself.

'I'll wait till you're upstairs – as usual.'

It was an old custom. When she was upstairs she would open her window and wave to him.

Only now did she show any real emotion. She tried to smile. Her lips trembled. Bartels looked quickly away, and walked through the doorway.

'Well, I'm off,' he said. Outside, he turned round and said: 'Well, good-bye, Lorna.' He hesitated a second; he wanted to add: 'Good-bye, darling.' But he didn't.

She stood in the doorway while the Corgi walked past her into the warmth of the house. She raised her hand and waved; it was a confused, feeble little movement. She said nothing.

That was the last picture he had of her, standing in the doorway while the Corgi dog walked past her. Then she closed the door.

He walked to the little garden gate and waited as usual. The light went out in the porch. The light went out in the drawing-room, and in the hall, and he thought: she is going up the stairs now.

The light went on in her bedroom.

He waited for half a minute, wondering whether she would open the window; holding his cigarette ready to wave to her, as he had always done in the past.

But the window remained shut. A sob of self-pity rose in his throat.

*

He drove along the lane as fast as possible in third gear, to warm up the engine, swung into the main road, and changed into top.

Where the road filtered into the main London–Guildford road he slowed down, dropped into Cobham, drove along the winding road through Cobham, and then accelerated up to fifty.

The snow still lay on the grass verges and partly cloaked the hedges, but the continual traffic had mostly cleared the road itself. He drove with the car astride one of the lanes of cat's eyes, and the long lines of little reflector studs, looming up endlessly out of the darkness ahead, threw back the light of his headlamps so that he had the impression of a continuous stream of tracer bullets entering the body of the car, entering his own body causing the pain which dragged interminably at his inside.

There was not a great deal of traffic about. The night air and the temperature, still below freezing point, had kept most people indoors. But now and again he passed a car, and occasionally a coach, the windows misted up, the interior alight and suggestive of warmth and human company. Bartels, in the dark interior of his car, alone with his fear, thought again of the letters he had written.

'Never put anything on paper, old boy,' that's what they had said, the knowing ones in the Army; the ones who boasted of their conquests, in the Mess; the love-spivs, and fly Casanovas, the speculators in fornication, and the gamblers in the dicey game of adultery. Tell 'em what you like, but don't put it on paper, old boy . . . no letters, old boy, no letters . . . women always keep 'em . . . fatal. The damnable thing was that they were right, and he had been wrong.

A good opportunity to do it. To do what? Murder, of course, that's what any jury would say. *That which we both know has to be done.* What? Murder, obviously: he and Lorna in the dock: Lorna looking at the Judge, unafraid. Blue-grey eyes and firm chin. Unafraid, because she believed in British Justice.

No innocent person is ever hanged in England, people said.

Better that a hundred guilty persons should escape than

that one innocent person be punished unjustly. That's what people said.

Justice, British justice, world renowned, and a jury, doing its best, but swayed by the instincts and prejudices inherited over the centuries: respectable men and women trying to rid their minds of the knowledge that Lorna was the third point in the eternal triangle.

What chance had the Other Woman on a murder charge before ten respectable men and two respectable housewives?

Before he found the answer, he saw the dark car as it slid past him, and took no notice of it, but pulled further in to the side of the road to let it go by. He always kept an eye on his driving mirror, and he had seen no car behind him.

It must have been following him without sidelights, or else it must have swooped upon him out of a side road where it had been lurking.

The bell throbbed loud and clear as the dark car passed, and speeded up, and then drew in to the side of the road some yards ahead. Now he saw the 'police' sign, illuminated above the roof, and a hand waving him to slow down and stop.

So soon, Beatrice dead so soon.

But it wasn't fair. They shouldn't have known he was on this road. Even if they had found her, and had found the number of his car, they shouldn't have known he was on this road. They shouldn't have been able to diagnose the cause of death so soon.

A question leaped at him out of the darkness, suddenly and without warning. What proof was there that Beatrice, a human being, would react to the drug in the same way as the dog Brutus? He gripped the steering-wheel to fight down his fears.

Subsidiary questions crowded in upon him. Supposing the book on poisons had been wrong? Supposing she had managed to reach the phone before she lost consciousness? People react differently to drugs.

Supposing she had had her moment of fear after all, her seconds of terror; like the attack of palpitations, only ten times worse, and in her panic had called out his name: 'Barty!' Perhaps she had called a second time, instinctively, even though aware that he was not there: 'Barty! I feel so queer, Barty!'

Calling to him for help, calling to her murderer, in implicit faith, and staggering to dial '999', and dying in fear and pain after all, like the butterfly in the flames.

His heart throbbed in his throat. He had an absurd urge to ignore the signal, to sweep past the police, and on for a few yards, and then make a wild break across the fields.

But he pulled up behind the police car, and lowered the window by the driving-seat, and sat waiting while a wave of nausea swept over him. Two officers got out of the police car and walked towards him. One stood in front of the car, and wrote down his registration number in a book. The other came up to the car, and bent down and put his face through the window.

'Are you aware that you have no rear light, sir?'

'No rear light?' whispered Bartels. 'No rear light?'

'No, sir. Perhaps you would care to get out and confirm what I have said?'

They want to see if I'm sober, thought Bartels, they want to see me walk to the rear of the car, and see whether I walk properly. Perhaps he smelt the whisky on my breath. I must be careful not to slip on the icy road as I get out; slip and fall to the ground; I must be careful not to slip as I walk to the rear of the car; I must walk carefully, but not too carefully; I mustn't hold on to the side of the car, even though I might normally do so on a road like this. That would look bad. If they take me in charge, it is the end. And I must not enunciate my words too carefully when I talk to them. That would be bad, too. Mustn't speak too carefully, and mustn't speak thickly. If I'm arrested, Beatrice will die, be consumed in the flames as the butterfly was burnt in the grate.

Bartels opened the door and got out. He walked slowly but steadily to the rear of the car.

The police officer pointed. 'See, sir? No light.'

Bartels gave the light a bang with his hand, and the bulb lit up.

'That's better,' said the police officer.

'Bad connexion,' said Bartels, and smiled.

'You were, of course, committing an offence, sir; you realize that?'

Bartels nodded. 'I suppose so.'

'Have you your driving licence with you, sir?'

'You're not going to report me for this, surely?'

'Have you your driving licence with you, sir?' the officer said again.

'Yes.'

Bartels felt in his pocket and took out the licence. The officer examined it, slowly and methodically, and entered some particulars in a note-book.

Oh, God, prayed Bartels, make him get a move on, make him hurry up: the minutes are passing. Oh, God, if You exist, make this man hurry.

The police officer handed back the licence. Bartels turned to get into his car again. The police officer said:

'Have you your certificate of insurance with you, sir?'

'I have, I assure you. And it's in order. Must you see it? I am in rather a hurry.'

In rather a hurry, that was bad. He shouldn't have said that. That was the sort of thing which is remembered. And on the night in question, members of the jury, he was seen to be in a distressed and agitated condition, both by the bar-tender of the hotel in Cobham, and by a police patrol who chanced to stop him. Bad, bad.

He heard the officer say: 'May I see it, sir?'

He took out his wallet and extracted the certificate of insurance. The man examined it and handed it back.

'Where are you coming from, sir?'

'Near Woking.'

'And your destination?'

'London.'

'That's all, thank you, sir. Good night.'

But from the other side of the car, the second officer suddenly said:

'Just one moment, sir. You don't appear to have a road-fund licence, properly displayed on the windscreen.'

'It's fallen off,' said Bartels.

He pulled open the door of the car and frantically felt for it on the floor by the front passenger seat.

'It's in a holder which is attached to the windscreen by suction, and it's an old one, and the rubber has perished, and it falls off now and again.'

He continued to grope in the darkness. 'Here it is,' he said at length.

The second officer examined it carefully.

'You know it's an offence to drive a vehicle without a roadfund licence properly displayed on the windscreen, sir?'

'Yes, but I had it. I had it with me. And it's in order.'

'It wasn't displayed, sir.'

'No,' said Bartels. 'It wasn't displayed.' His voice shook a little. How long had they wasted? Five minutes, ten minutes?

'I'll get it seen to,' added Bartels humbly. 'I'll get it seen to, tomorrow.'

'Better get a new one, sir,' said the second officer. 'That'd be the best in the long run, sir. Get a new one.'

'I'll get a new one tomorrow,' said Bartels desperately. 'Is that all?'

'That's all, sir. Good night.'

'Good night,' said Bartels.

He climbed back into the driving-seat. The officers walked back to their car. Bartels waited until the police car had started, watched it, as it slid swiftly forward, and saw the tail-light grow smaller in the distance.

He switched on his own engine, and drove on. It had begun to snow again, not continuously, but intermittently. Bartels switched on the windscreen wiper, and noted with relief that it was working again.

He drove more slowly for a mile or two, while he sorted things out in his mind. The incident had shaken him. He tried to think whether he had said or done anything he should not have done, apart from showing some impatience.

He didn't like their questions about where he was coming from, and what was his destination. He had told Beatrice he was going to Colchester. Supposing she had mentioned it to somebody else, and that came out, combined with the fact that he had now been officially noted as being on the road from Woking?

Why had he told her that lie? It was stupid and pointless. He could as well have said his dinner was in Woking.

One after another they cropped up, he thought, the unforeseeable little things which you cannot reasonably cater for. Everything seems simple and straightforward at first, but it isn't.

Sin is not simple. Virtue is simple but not easy, and sin is easy but not simple. Sin is tortuous and twisted, involving lies, and lies within lies, and the bending and warping of the conscience, and subterfuges and concealments, and the ever-present necessity to be on your guard, to watch your every action, to rein in your tongue, to act normally when you yearn to show emotion; only to discover that in acting, as you thought, in a normal manner, you have in fact acted abnormally.

He was half way between Cobham and Esher, and saw by the dashboard clock that it was twenty minutes to ten. He began to calculate.

The Kingston By-pass took thirteen minutes, at night, he knew that one; from the London end of the by-pass to his flat took not more than twenty-minutes, that totalled thirty-three minutes.

He had to be back by 10.30 at the latest, which meant that he had seventeen minutes to reach Esher, pass through Esher, and reach the by-pass which was a couple of minutes' drive further on.

He had ample time, provided Beatrice adhered to her routine, and at the moment when he came to this conclusion he knew without a shadow of doubt that he would not reach his flat, after all, not by 10.30 or even by 11.30.

Something would stop him.

Something would reach out of the night around him, something which was watching him now, with a laugh in its throat; observing him drop speed from fifty miles an hour to forty-five, and then to forty; smiling to see him peer through the windscreen at the road ahead.

It, or its minion, lurked in every side-turning, ready to shoot out at him in splintering collision; sat at the wheel of each oncoming car, drunk and unfit to be driving; laid its hand upon the over-burdened boughs of the snow-covered trees under which he passed, ready to drop a branch in his path.

It wasn't even snowing now, and he stopped the windscreen wiper, and the road ahead lay clear and white in the moonlight, but Bartels knew that that made no difference to the inevitable end. He dropped speed still further, to thirty-five miles an hour, and slowed down at each side-turning; and hugged the side of the road when a lorry rumbled up from behind and passed him and thundered on.

He drove carefully, tense and alert, but he knew it made no difference because he knew now that the something which would reach out for him would not take such obvious forms as he had imagined.

He knew it, because each time he took some precaution he heard it giggle delightedly in his ear, like a sadistic young schoolboy torturing a frog.

He knew it would not operate through an engine defect, or a mechanical defect of any kind; nor through a puncture, or a tyre burst. Nothing so prosaic as that.

He crawled through Esher at twenty miles an hour, and when he had passed through the town, and came to the first traffic roundabout on the way back, and joined the by-pass, he felt better.

His nerve returned, and he increased speed.

There was no more giggling in his ear; the schoolboy stood back, the frog made off afresh. There was nothing to fear now, except time.

The by-pass stretched ahead, broad, sometimes gently curving, well illuminated in the appropriate places, and properly controlled by traffic lights and roundabouts. There were no side-turnings where danger could lurk, and ample room for cars to pass.

When he came to the double carriage-way, he increased speed to fifty. He felt ashamed of the time he had wasted through his over-cautious driving, but not unhopeful that he would arrive home with a quarter of an hour or more to spare.

Beatrice rarely started going to bed before 10.30 or 10.45; sometimes not till 11.15. He pictured himself going into the flat, greeting her as she sat by the fire having her final cup of weak China tea. Then casually going into the bedroom, and taking the bottle from the bedside.

After that, he would have to throw the altrapeine down the drain in the bathroom, and wash out the bottle and throw it in the dustbin, or put it in his overcoat pocket; it would be of no further importance, anyway.

The one he had bought at lunch-time, the one containing the remains of pure stomach powder, he would leave by the bedside. If she was in the bedroom he would announce that he had left the dinner early because he had not been feeling very well, and ask if he could have the remains of her medicine. She would certainly agree. He smiled at how easy it would be.

The frog was getting uppish, now.

The path of sin was not so tortuous after all, it was straightening out nicely, and as to the future, as to Lorna, that, too, could be considered in due course. He passed the second and third roundabouts, thinking of sin, and the Seven Deadly Sins, which are said to be Pride, Covetousness, Lust, Gluttony, Anger, Envy, and Sloth; and he tried to discover which it was that had led him to his present position.

He was not proud; indeed, in some ways he was rather meek. He did not covet Lorna, because covetousness involved desiring that which belonged to somebody else, and Lorna belonged to nobody.

He did not lust after her, either; his feelings were too gentle, too tender, and above all too protective; and the rest of the Seven Deadly Sins did not seem to come into the picture.

What, then, had been the driving force?

He wondered if the secret lay in some sort of secondary products of the Seven Deadly Sins, and toyed with the thought in a morbid desire to lay bare the basic defect in his character.

He tried to persuade himself that in wishing to shelter Lorna from the difficulties of the world, he was in reality wishing to see himself as the knight errant, the recipient of her gratitude and praise ; a desire which was possibly a watery by-product of pride and lust. By the bonds of marriage, he belonged to Beatrice, yet he wished to belong to Lorna: was this, in some twisted, inverted form, a manifestation of covetousness? He shook his head. It was all far-fetched and unconvincing.

Far ahead, he could see the lights of the fifth roundabout, and glanced at the clock and saw that he was now making good time.

He reverted to the consideration of lust, because it was something to do, something to keep his mind off what he might find when he got home.

Expressed in its simplest form the position was that he, Bartels, wanted a certain woman. To get her, he was prepared to kill. That was it, there you had it: you had to put from your mind the excuses, the consoling thoughts of doing things for Lorna's good. You were not conscious of lust, of any overwhelming carnal desires, but the mere fact that you were prepared to kill to get her indicated that they were there in your subconscious.

But what of the much-extolled virtues of pity and mercy? If it were not for pity and mercy, he thought bitterly, I could have walked out on Beatrice like millions of other husbands have done in the past, and will do in the future.

The scandal would be short-lived, and you don't go to prison for it. They don't hang you for it. But they hang you if you kill your wife just because you have so much pity in you that you cannot leave her in loneliness.

If things went wrong, he would be ranked with Crippen. He would be portrayed as a callous monster in the eyes of posterity. But who knows what went on in the mind of the little man called Crippen? Who knows? thought Bartels again.

He was drawing near to the fifth roundabout when he

thought of how he would feel if he were put in prison, perhaps not even hanged, just put in prison, for years, behind locked doors.

Shut in, in a tiny cell, for hours on end each day and night. So that the walls pressed in on you, and the ceiling pressed down upon you, nearer and nearer, and closer and closer, and you could bang on the door and break the skin on your hands, and scream yourself hoarse, and it did not avail. And when the lights went out, there was the darkness, thick and cloying, and that suffocated you; and what with the darkness and the walls, you knew you were not really in a prison at all.

You were buried alive.

You were in your coffin, deep under the earth, slowly suffocating to death, in the darkness and the loneliness and the silence of the earth. Nobody would release you because nobody could hear you, and everybody thought you were dead, and nobody knew the doctor had made a mistake, and you had merely been in a cataleptic trance; feeling yourself being put in a shroud, and hearing the coffin lid come down, and feeling the swaying motion of the coffin-bearers, and the sound of the earth falling remorselessly above your head; falling, and falling, and falling, more and ever more of it, till the sounds grew fainter and only the silence remained.

He was shivering again now, fighting against the old, the dark shocking terrors, his hands wet upon the wheel.

He was near to the roundabout, when the black cat, emblem of good luck, but young and inexperienced, ran swiftly across the road before his car. Its ears were laid back, its tail arched like a squirrel's.

For a second he had glimpsed the young cat's eyes, green fire in the light of his head-lamps, and then it was in front of him.

Bartels didn't run it over.

He might have done so, had he had time to think it all out, but he acted instinctively, as he was bound to do, in the only way in which he, Philip Bartels, could have been expected to act.

Bartels braked.

If there had not been any snow, it might have been all right. If the coach, approaching from the right, with its lighted interior, had been a few minutes earlier, or later, it might not have been so bad, either.

As the car swung round in a circle, darted sideways, hit the 'Turn Left' sign, he heard the screaming of the coach brakes, and saw it swerve ineffectually, and crash with its fender into his own car, and felt the stab of pain in his side. It was only then that he felt afraid.

Even then it was only for a second.

He saw it looming over him, and heard the crash, and felt the pain, and hazily noted the strange stillness which followed for a brief moment the noise of the impact.

Before he lost consciousness he heard himself murmur: 'Beatrice', and was faintly surprised.

*

Extract from a police report prepared by Inspector Macdonald, of the Metropolitan Police Force, and shown to me, Peter Harding, in confidence, at a later date:

On 26 February, at about 10.40 p.m., as a result of a telephone message to the effect that Beatrice Bartels, a married woman, of 34, Alvington Court, W.8, was in danger of unknowingly taking a draught of medicine containing some poisonous substance, namely altrapeine, or that she may already have taken such medicine, I proceeded to the address in question, accompanied by Sergeant Wellings of this station, where I observed through a glass panel in the front door that a light appeared to be burning in the flat.

I rang the bell and knocked, but received no answer.

In view of the nature of the message which had been received, I instructed Sergeant Wellings to force an entry. This was effected by breaking a portion of the glass panel, and releasing the latch from inside.

An inspection of the flat showed that it was empty.

At 10.55 p.m. a woman who subsequently proved to be Mrs Bartels entered the flat, stating that she had been to the cinema and had left the light burning to discourage burglars.

I said to her: 'A man called Philip Bartels, who states that he is your husband, has been involved in a motor-car accident and is lying seriously injured in Richmond Hospital. This man has caused a message to be sent to the police to the effect that a poisonous substance, namely altrapeine, has been introduced into some medicine which he anticipated you would take before retiring to bed this evening.'

Mrs Bartels replied: 'There must be some mistake. I do not understand.'

I then said to her: 'Did you, in fact, intend to take some medicine before retiring this evening?'

She replied: 'Yes.'

I asked her where this medicine was to be found, and she replied: 'It is beside my bed.'

I went with her into a bedroom, and on a table by the side of the bed I saw a bottle containing a small amount of white powder. I informed Mrs Bartels that it would be necessary for me to remove the bottle and contents for examination, and she replied: 'Is that really necessary?'

I informed her again that it was necessary, and she made no reply. I then asked Mrs Bartels if she wanted to visit her husband in hospital, in view of his condition, and she replied: 'Later, perhaps. Not just now.' She was in a distressed state.

I left Sergeant Wellings with Mrs Bartels, and returned to this station, where, in view of the verbal statement already made by the husband, Philip Bartels, I made arrangements for police officers to attend Richmond Hospital with a view to taking any further statement from Bartels which he might care to make, and should he be in a position to make one.

Bartels lapsed into unconsciousness again during the night, but at 6.30 a.m., approximately, he recovered consciousness and made the statement which is attached to this report, but which he was not in a fit enough condition to sign.

Thus far, the police report was accurate. But the rest of it was inaccurate, on one particular, at least, which is why I said, at the beginning of this record of the affair, that one other person thought he knew all about the case, whereas in fact he didn't. Inspector Macdonald thought he had it all tidied up in his file, in view of Bartels' statement.

He was wrong.

Chapter 18

THERE was no daylight left now, but beyond the château a round harvest moon hung above the horizon, immense and golden, its rays dappling the path in the wood, the silent wood, where I had walked and laughed and loved in my youth.

I no longer wished to be alone.

I wanted company now, and lights, and talk, and maybe some hard liquor; not wine, with its gentle, mellowing effect, but something that worked fast, that would remove the gooseflesh that races over a man's skin when he is alone in a wood with thoughts like mine, when the shadows and the trees merge into shapes that are not the shapes of men but of things to which one cannot easily put a name.

The fact is, I did not wish to look again at the end of the affair. I wished that I did not have to amend the end of the Inspector's report. I would have liked the end of that report to have been the whole truth, instead of only part of the truth.

So far, I could raise arguments to prove that I had acted no worse than Bartels. Bartels had betrayed Beatrice, and I, in my turn, had betrayed Bartels. I had succeeded, and Bartels had failed, as he did all his life.

I could at least argue that, but for me, Lorna would not have changed her mind, Beatrice would have died and Bartels might have been hanged.

Chapter 19

HAD Bartels been a normally strong-looking fellow, I do not think I would have acted as I did, but he looked pathetic in that hospital bed, with the big, healthy detective sitting by the bedside. They had pulled the bed somewhat away from the wall, so that the detective sat discreetly behind the line of Bartels' vision.

They had put a screen round his bed, too, and he lay there with his head and chest and left arm swathed in bandages.

He had, they told me, a fractured base of the skull, together with two broken ribs and considerable bruising and laceration of the head and right side.

There was a risk of a haemorrhage of blood to the brain with fatal results, and he would be in danger for some days.

'He would not normally be allowed visitors,' said the ward sister, in a cool, tinny voice, 'However, he seemed to be unable to settle down until he had seen you.' She looked at me disapprovingly and added: 'You mustn't stay more than a few minutes.'

I nodded, and walked down the ward to the bed where he lay.

He opened his eyes when I placed my hand on his, and smiled his wide, thin-lipped smile.

'This is a pretty pickle,' he whispered, and I saw the police officer lean forward, note-book in hand, to catch his words.

'Get better,' I said. 'Then we'll sort things out.'

'It'll take some sorting out.'

His spectacles had been smashed in the accident, and he gazed up at me short-sightedly. For lack of anything better to say, I repeated: 'Get better, first, Barty.'

He closed his eyes for a few seconds, and I wondered if he had fallen asleep. But he opened them after a while and said:

'I wonder if Beatrice will ever understand. I don't suppose so. Poor Beatrice.'

I sought round desperately for something to say to distract his thoughts from Beatrice.

'I'm afraid your car's a bit of a mess,' I said inanely.

He smiled faintly. 'So am I.'

'You'll be all right,' I said.

He closed his eyes again, and his mind reverted to Beatrice, and when he spoke his voice was so low that I joined the police officer in bending down to catch his words.

'Tell her, try to explain to her, that I only acted out of pity. Didn't want her to suffer, you know.' He sighed and added: 'Pity. Bad thing, pity. Much better to be normal, like you, Pete.'

'I'll tell her,' I answered. 'I'll tell her, Barty. She'll understand. She's a very intelligent girl.'

He nodded, almost imperceptibly. 'Very intelligent girl, Pete. Tell her what I said.'

He remained quiet for fully half a minute, then sighed again, and added: 'But I doubt if she will understand. It's a bit too much to ask.'

I saw the police officer scribbling in his note-book.

A nurse put her head round the door, and made signs that I would have to leave. I put my hand on his again.

'I must go now, Barty. You've got to have plenty of rest.'

He suddenly opened his eyes, then, and stared at me.

To my horror I realized that they were filled with fear, and his pallor had been transformed by a sudden rush of blood to his face. I had seen him look like that before.

There was the same wild look as I had seen when they threw the rug over his head at the picnic at the château; the same terrified look which Mary, the American girl, must have seen the evening when we had locked them both into a bedroom; and the same piteous, frightened expression as I had seen, in those almost forgotten schooldays, when we had pushed him under the vaulting horse in the gymnasium during the singing lessons.

But I didn't think of all that then. I only saw the terror. I didn't know what was the matter. I didn't think he was afraid of dying, and I was right, but I couldn't guess what was in his mind. I increased my pressure on his hand.

'What's up, Barty?' I asked, softly.

'Locked doors,' he whispered.

I looked round. There were no locked doors, as far as I could see. There was only a screen round the bed, and even then there was a wide gap between the screen and the wall.

'They won't understand,' he murmured.

'Who won't?'

He shook his head, while the fear burned and blazed in his eyes, and I felt his hand grow damp and hot in mine.

'They'll put me in prison, Pete.'

I saw the police officer begin to scribble again in his notebook. 'Locked doors, and pitch darkness at night. I can't stand it, Pete. I'd rather die than that.'

I saw the police officer bending nearer, anxious not to miss a word. I felt Bartels' hand beneath my own begin to clench and twist and pull at the bedclothes. I gripped it harder still, and stared at him groping for something to say.

As I searched in my mind for some words of comfort, I heard him murmur to me to bend closer. I put my head down, and he said:

'Put your ear against my lips, Pete.'

Out of the corner of my eye, I saw the police officer draw as close as he could. But Bartels only said five words: 'Altrapeine – please, Pete. Please, Pete.'

I raised my head, and caught the police officer's eye, and saw the question forming on his lips.

'All right,' I said in a normal, loud voice. 'All right, I'll see what I can do.'

The fear slowly seeped from Bartels' face. Now there was only a mute, sad appeal in his eyes. I got up, and picked up my hat.

'Tomorrow?' murmured Bartels.

'I'll come and see you tomorrow, if you're well enough,' I replied in the soothing tones one uses to sick people. 'Now get some rest, Barty.'

I went out, round the screen, and had begun to walk down the ward, when I heard footsteps behind me, and felt a hand on my arm. I looked round and saw it was the police officer.

'May I have a word with you outside, sir?'

'If you wish.'

We walked to the door, and stopped in the passage outside the ward.

'I must ask you what he said to you, sir.'

He stood in front of me, tall and solidly built, healthily red in the face. His hair was cut very short above the ears, his brown eyes were alert and restless. They were the eyes of a person who is accustomed to watch the faces of others for reactions, for the tell-tale flicker of the eyes, the movement of the mouth which indicates dismay; the eyes of a man accustomed to dominate; eyes which did not waver, but nevertheless moved and roamed over the face of the person to whom he was talking. They were not exactly hostile, but neither were they sympathetic or friendly.

I thought, by way of contrast, of Bartels' eyes, so full of fear, so filled with silent appeal. I had a swift mental vision of a host of other eyes, hard, implacable eyes gazing at Bartels in the years to come. Police officers' eyes, warders' eyes, newspapermen's eyes in Court, warders' eyes again, fellow convicts' eyes. Gazing at him as he panicked in his cell, gazing at him in the dock, and again, through the years, in his cell.

I think it was at that moment that I decided to do as Bartels wished.

'It was nothing to do with your investigation,' I answered, and made as if to pass him; but he stood solidly in my way.

'I see, sir.' He tapped his teeth with the chewed end of a pencil.

He made no move. 'Well?' I said.

'I take it that in that case you would have no objection to telling me what he said, sir.'

Again I was conscious of his eyes, unbelieving and unyielding, roaming over my face. I react rather brusquely to that sort of thing.

'Actually, I would,' I said abruptly.

'May I ask why, sir?' Police officers always seem to call you 'sir' a great deal. It doesn't mean a thing.

'For personal reasons.' I saw his hard mouth tighten.

'There is an offence known as obstructing a police officer in the course of his duty.'

I laughed, then, at this bluff, and saw his eyes flinch.

'Who is obstructing whom at this moment?' He ignored the question.

'I take it sir, that you decline to say what he told you, sir?'

We looked at each other for a full ten seconds, eye to eye, in silence. I sighed.

'All right, if you really insist. Do you?'

'It would be helpful, sir.'

The expression on his face relaxed. I could read his thoughts as though he had spoken them aloud: firmness, he was thinking, firmness – that's what counts. They always come clean.

'He asked me to pray for him,' I said. 'He asked me to go into a church and pray for him.'

*

I went into my darkroom, and stared at the row of bottles, and in particular at the altrapeine bottle. I knew, of course, little about the case, except that it was known that something of a poisonous nature had been placed in Beatrice's medicine bottle, and that Bartels had apparently put it there. So much the Inspector had told me, edging round the subject in the way the police do when they are not certain of the reliability of the person they are questioning.

Now I could guess what the poison was. Later, when I had become very friendly with the Inspector, and read Bartels' statement, I learnt where and how he bought it.

It was eight o'clock in the morning when the Inspector had called. He had taken his statement from Beatrice Bartels and he had then come to me. He had asked for the names of any of Bartels' friends, and mine had headed the list.

I told him a great deal about Bartels, but nothing about Lorna Dickson. I guessed Bartels would not have mentioned her. I saw no reason why I should. Beatrice had not died. There was no call for society to revenge itself for a murder which never took place, or for Lorna to be involved.

Maybe, I was wrong, but that is the way I thought.

I saw the Inspector inching nearer to the subject of a mistress as a motive, and mentally stood back and admired his technique.

First, he asked what particular friends might help to throw any light on the affair. I told him that I did not think any of Bartels' friends could.

Then he said that doubtless there would be one or two broken hearts in the provinces if Bartels died, and when I looked at him and pretended to seem puzzled, he said slyly: 'Well, you know what they say about commercial travellers, sir. Not that I'd be one to frown on a little innocent larking now and again.'

When that failed, he asked point blank if Bartels had any liaison outside the bonds of marriage. But I was ready for him by then.

'None, as far as I know,' I said, looking him full in the face. 'None at all. I always considered him to be devoted to his wife.'

So after my visit to the hospital I stood gazing at the altrapeine bottle in the darkroom, pondering that which Bartels had planned. Although some time had elapsed, I still felt numbed by the shock of events. As yet they made little sense, because I had not yet understood the fatal weakness which was his downfall.

I saw a gently, kindly little man who had plotted a ruthless, diabolical murder, and the apparent and appalling contradiction bewildered me.

Only later was I able to realize that, in fact, there was no contradiction at all; that it was pity, kindness, and humanity which drove Bartels to his doom. Without those three virtues, without their unbalancing effect upon a sensitive and delicate mind, there would have been no attempted murder.

At that time, however, it all seemed so unnecessary.

I could see no reason why he could not just leave Beatrice; those of us who are in the hotel business are inclined to regard such actions as unfortunate, perhaps, but commonplace enough.

I had not had time, either, to look back over the years and see how the lack of love in his youth had made him so crave it in later years that he was prepared to kill to win it.

After a while, I went out of the darkroom, but I did not

take the poison bottle with me. I went out of my flat, and along to the reference room of the public library, and there made certain researches among the medical books.

In the end, I came to the same conclusion about altrapeine as that at which Bartels had arrived. I went back to the flat, and heated up some of the coffee left over from breakfast, and took it into the drawing-room.

I drank three cups of coffee, black and very sweet, one after the other, sipping them slowly, and trying to erase certain pictures from my mind, but at the end of the third cup, I knew that I would not succeed.

I told myself that even in prison a man could receive expert psychological treatment. But cold reason could not efface the actualities I had seen. It could not wipe from the heart the distress caused by the wild, pitiful appeal which had flamed in the eyes of Bartels as he lay in the hospital bed, with the red-faced detective sitting by his side: the trapped bird, caught in the legal net, broadcasting, without any attempt at concealment, the waves of its fear, beating against the net, hopelessly and monstrously stripped of all dignity and pride.

What fears were these, and how incomprehensible to the normal person, that they should cause a man to lose his self-respect, cause his eyes to dilate wildly, and his face to flush, and his hand to crush and twist a counterpane!

I, who have been blessed by nature with a more stolid temperament, who have known but little fear in my life, tried in vain to capture a hint of such terrors.

I only knew they existed, because I had seen the look on Bartels' face. I had seen some such look upon the face of a gravely wounded soldier before the doctor arrived with the merciful dose of morphine.

I saw no such release for Bartels.

Indeed, I saw no mercy for him at all, but only the seas of panic, and the long dark years in the long grey corridors;

and the sense of the loss of Lorna Dickson; and the burden of the knowledge of failure.

I lit a cigarette and considered the practical side of the matter. I told myself that Bartels was a fool, and I was even more of a fool to risk disgrace and punishment for his sake.

Nevertheless, I fetched the altrapeine bottle and made my plans. They were simple enough.

I went to the hospital in the late afternoon of the following day, as the light was fading. The sister in charge informed me that Bartels had had a restless night, but that failing a sudden relapse his chance of recovery were reasonable.

The same detective was on duty, and he greeted me with a curt nod. I knew that this man was an antagonist, that I had to be careful of him, but I felt cool enough, and I held, in my left hand the small flat paper packet, open at one end, so that its contents would slide forth easily.

I would like to be able to record that my last talk with Philip Bartels had a hidden drama unperceived by the detective with his mackintosh and his horrible note-book, and chewed pencil, and his hard, alert eyes, and his slightly protruding ears; that it contained obscure phrases of significance to both of us.

Such was not the case.

I sat by the side of his bed, on a hard chair.

'How are you feeling?' I asked.

He nodded and smiled. 'I've felt worse.'

'Is there anything you want, Barty? Fruit? Can you eat fruit?'

'Not yet,' he murmured. 'No fruit yet.'

'Are they treating you well?'

'Quite well,' he murmured.

'It's still bitterly cold outside,' I said. He nodded.

'And Beatrice?' he asked softly.

'I've not seen Beatrice yet. Her mother has come up.'

'Have any of the others heard?'

'Nobody,' I said. 'Nobody at all.'

He seemed content, and closed his eyes for a while. The detective put his note-book down and relaxed. A gust of wind blew against the windows and rattled them, and the sound caused Bartels to open his eyes.

He said nothing, but held my eyes with his own. The detective, now that the conversation had lapsed, sat picking at a button on his mackintosh, inattentive and bored.

I had to know whether Bartels had changed his mind, and raised my eyebrows in silent question. Because of his short sight, I doubt if he saw, but he smiled slightly and nodded. He looked peaceful and contented, like a child who, after lamentations and protests, is now tucked up in bed and warm and reconciled. Indeed, he looked happier at that moment than I had seen him look for months. It was as though all his personal problems were resolved. Having no future he had no worries. He was about to leave the world, which had proved too much for him, and he was not sorry.

He raised his hand to his forehead, and then carelessly placed it near the side-table, the forefinger pointing, as if by chance, to the plastic tumbler, containing water.

Now, for the first time, I felt tense and keyed up, I knew that Bartels would make the opening gambit, and that I would have to follow.

It came quite suddenly:

'Pete?'

'Yes,' I said, and saw the detective begin to pay attention again.

'Could you get me a little more water out of the tap?'

I got up and took the plastic tumbler. It was still half-full, and although the light in the room was heavily shaded, I placed my hand round the tumbler lest the detective should see the level of the water through the thin material.

I walked over to the hand-basin and ran the water for a moment, keeping my left hand on the tap. I ran a little water into the mug, and tipped my left hand so that the white powder flowed into the mug.

I turned off the tap, and walked back to the bed.

'Are you sure you want a drink, Barty?'

He nodded. 'If you don't mind. I'm so sorry to trouble you,' he added. He put out his hand for the mug, but I shook my head.

'Let me hold it for you,' I said. I raised his head with my left hand, and put the tumbler to his lips. I was conscious of hearing the detective speak. I heard him above the beating of my heart, and was irritated; he said something about Bartels not being supposed to drink too much.

Bartels emptied the tumbler.

I said: 'I'll refill it, in case you need some more later.' I rinsed out the receptacle, twice, added some water, and replaced it on the side table.

'You shouldn't have let him drink all that,' said the detective peevishly.

'No,' I said. 'No, perhaps I was wrong.'

Bartels looked up at me from his pillow. He said:

'I think perhaps you had better go, Pete. Thanks for everything. I feel a little tired. I think I'll sleep.'

I stood up and looked down at him.

'Well, so-long, Barty,' I said. 'Good luck.'

He said nothing more, but lay with his eyes closed.

'Visits tire him,' said the detective, pulling a cheap, paper-backed edition of some novel from his mackintosh pocket and beginning to read. I doubt if he even saw Bartels die.

*

First I heard the sound of the Americans' car on the distant Orléans-Blois highway, then the engine noise died away as it slowed to turn into the poplar drive, then the sound increased as it accelerated up the drive.

I could not see it at first, because the château lay between me and the drive, but eventually I saw the light from the headlamps reflected from the trees at the side of the house, and then, once again, there was only the soft moonlight.

I slipped deeper into the wood, and walked softly along the path which led past the château, and past the ruined tennis-courts. Behind me I heard men talking and a woman laugh. I walked more quickly, and once, as something stirred in the undergrowth by the side of the path, I felt the gooseflesh again run over my skin.

I rounded each bend in the path with a conscious effort, each time afraid lest I should see before me a figure on the path. The sweet, nostalgic melancholy of the sunset hours had departed, and loneliness and apprehension had taken its place.

I wanted no more of the château, and knew that I would never visit it again. I had thought that it would hold for me nothing but the tender memories of youthful happiness, that here Bartels and I, and Beatrice, and Ingrid, and all the rest of that cheerful crowd could meet within the compass of my mind, and be reunited for an hour or so, and talk and walk and laugh and love as we had done in the days gone by.

But it didn't work out that way.

Fear became mixed with the joy, and remorse and self-reproach stretched out their long, strong fingers and smeared the images. I suppose there is always that risk if you revisit a place where you think you can regain for a while your earlier rapture.

Moreover, one small doubt remained unresolved.

I thought of it as I made my way along the side of the drive, and to where my car stood, its sidelights unlit, a menace to all on the highway.

I thought of it as I drove back to Orléans, and again later, when they asked me whether I had enjoyed 'my sentimental journey', as they called it.

I said I had, of course, though the doubt still nagged at me, and they laughed indulgently. Only Lorna, dear Lorna, my wife, did not laugh, did not even smile; for Lorna had advised me not to go.

My doubt is, I suppose, a case of scruples.

It is due to the fact that as I held the tumbler to Bartels' lips, and watched him drink, a thought flashed through my mind which I tried instantly to suppress.

The thought was: 'He'll never kiss her with those lips again. She's safe now, beyond all risk or doubt: she's mine.'

I wish the thought had never occurred to me. But it cannot be helped now. I am, as I have indicated, a worldly type, little prone to introspection. The memory of that thought will grow fainter.

I won Lorna, and what I win I hold, and nothing, not even the shades of Philip Bartels, shall ever come between us: I was always a better man than Bartels, better at everything, including murder.

NOTE

Although a poison such as the one mentioned in this story exists, it is not considered to be in the public interest to enable it to be identified. It has therefore been given a fictitious name.

The main purpose in mentioning this is to save discontented husbands the trouble of searching fruitlessly through medical books.

J.B.

MORE ABOUT PENGUINS, PELICANS
AND PUFFINS

For further information about books available from Penguins please write to Dept EP, Penguin Books Ltd, Harmondsworth, Middlesex UB7 0DA.

In the U.S.A.: For a complete list of books available from Penguins in the United States write to Dept DG, Penguin Books, 299 Murray Hill Parkway, East Rutherford, New Jersey 07073.

In Canada: For a complete list of books available from Penguins in Canada write to Penguin Books Canada Limited, 2801 John Street, Markham, Ontario L3R 1B4.

In Australia: For a complete list of books available from Penguins in Australia write to the Marketing Department, Penguin Books Australia Ltd, P.O. Box 257, Ringwood, Victoria 3134.

In New Zealand: For a complete list of books available from Penguins in New Zealand write to the Marketing Department, Penguin Books (N.Z.) Ltd, Private Bag, Takapuna, Auckland 9.

In India: For a complete list of books available from Penguins in India write to Penguin Overseas Ltd, 706 Eros Apartments, 56 Nehru Place, New Delhi 110019.

Also by John Bingham

MY NAME IS MICHAEL SIBLEY

'I was always rather brave about Prosset when he was a long way away.'

Now Prosset is a very long way away, quite dead. Sibley had always secretly hated the domineering Prosset, especially at school. In fact, recently he had really wanted to kill him, with good reason too.

So how can he now sign his first police statement with the confidence that he had nothing to do with Prosset's grisly come-uppance?

It was with this unnerving and compelling novel that the great John Bingham made his debut – the classic crime writer who would much later be revealed as Lord Clanmorris of MI5.

'The most exciting story about a man involved in a sudden death I have read since the brilliant tales of Francis Iles' – Dennis Wheatley

PENGUIN CLASSIC CRIME

The Big Knockover and Other Stories   Dashiell Hammett
With these sharp, spare, laconic stories, Hammett invented a
new folk hero – the private eye. 'Dashiell Hammett gave
murder back to the kind of people that commit it for
reasons, not just to provide a corpse; and with the means at
hand, not with handwrought duelling pistols, curare, and
tropical fish' – Raymond Chandler

Death of a Ghost   Margery Allingham
A picture painted by a dead artist leads to murder . . . and
Albert Campion has to face his dearest enemy. With the skill
we have come to expect from one of the great crime writers
of all time, Margery Allingham weaves an enthralling web
of murder, intrigue and suspense.

Fen Country   Edmund Crispin
Dandelions and hearing aids, a bloodstained cat, a Leonardo
drawing, a corpse with an alibi, a truly poisonous letter . . .
these are just some of the unusual clues that Oxford don/
detective Gervase Fen is confronted with in this sparkling
collection of short mystery stories by one of the great
masters of detective fiction. 'The mystery fan's ideal bedside
book' – *Kirkus Reviews*

The Wisdom of Father Brown   G. K. Chesterton
Twelve delightful stories featuring the world's most beloved
amateur sleuth. Here Father Brown's adventures take him
from London to Cornwall, from Italy to France. He becomes involved with bandits, treason, murder, curses, and
an American crime-detection machine.